PUBLIC GHOST NUMBER ONE

Ghosts of London 2

PUSS IN PRINT PUBLICATIONS

Public Ghost Number One

Ghosts of London 2

Copyright © 2016 by Nic Saint

All rights reserved. No part of this book may be reproduced in any form by any electronic or mechanical means including photocopying, recording, or information storage and retrieval without permission in writing from the author.

Edited by Chereese Graves

www.nicsaint.com

Give feedback on the book at:
info@nicsaint.com

facebook.com/nicsaintauthor
@nicsaintauthor

First Edition

Printed in the U.S.A

Chapter 1

Emmanuella Sheetenhelm—Em to her friends—was an exceedingly organized woman, her affairs always perfectly in order. Her apartment, like her personal appearance, was invariably immaculate. So when the incident occurred, it was safe to say she was more than a little annoyed.

Weird stuff only rarely happened in a life as controlled as Em's. Granted, she'd gone through a recent episode that could only be termed as weird, when an evil fiend had attacked both her and some friends of her son Darian. But then of course that was to be expected, since Darian was Scotland Yard, always busy chasing the dregs of humankind. Sometimes those dregs of humankind will strike back, and don't care who gets caught in the crossfire.

And as she sat cross-legged in her meditation space now, the sweet aroma of incense tickling her nose just the way she liked it, a small Buddha statue gleaming and beaming at her from the small altar she'd erected, and soft new age music filling the space, she had the distinct impression that either the CD was skipping again, or a second voice had joined the chorus.

She resisted the urge to open her eyes, knowing that nothing breaks a good meditation session as quickly as opening your eyes, but couldn't resist shaking her head in annoyance. Her curly platinum hair dangled loosely around her shoulders, and for the occasion she'd put on her newly bought Lululemon yoga outfit, the one she'd seen Miranda Kerr wear on TV: the Devotion Long-sleeve Tee, accessorized with the Intuition Sweater Wrap draped loosely around her shoulders. Her Donna Karan sweatpants, a deeper shade of salmon than the rest of her outfit, completed the picture of the perfect power meditator.

And as she tried to ignore the audio mishap and focused on her breathing instead, it happened again: a new voice, intruding upon her calm equilibrium and the inner peace and mindfulness she was striving for. The voice was singing horribly out of tune, adding words to the music she didn't think were appropriate at all. Things like, 'Horrible old woman!' and 'Just go away!'

She didn't think a CD called 'Yoga Sounds' should contain such phrases, and had a good mind to take it back to the store when a sudden putrid stench drowned out the delightful scent of her Satya Nag Champa incense sticks.

"Yuck!" she cried, wondering where the stink was coming from. Had she forgotten to close the window after her yoga session and was this London's way of reminding her she lived in the big city and not the countryside?

The smell was positively foul, as if something had died and come back, dragging its decaying, rotting corpse to collapse on her nice Oriental rug.

Reluctantly, she gave up on her meditation and opened her eyes. And it was then that she saw it: something horrid, slithering and slipping away into the wall just as she glanced over her shoulder. It left a big, wet spot of green right next to the bookcase where she kept her collection of Deepak Chopra, Shakti Gawain, and Eckhart Tolle books, and as she watched in agonized horror, she thought she could see a smudge of sludge on the floor as well.

"Oh, my God!" she cried, and as she spoke the words, the thing popped out of the bookcase again, and was now leering at her. "Oh. My. God!" she repeated as she got a good look at the uninvited visitor, and clasped a startled hand to her Intuition Sweater Wrap.

Whatever it was, it looked horrible! Its chalk-white face small and pinched, eyes red-rimmed and lips blue, it looked like the ghost of a little girl.

Em struggled to get to her feet, her legs wobbly after sitting cross-legged for so long. And as she scrambled back, she almost upset the Buddha and the candles she'd put there to afford the illumined one some extra illumination.

"Go away!" she now cried feebly, and would have held up a crucifix if she'd had one available. As it was, she wildly made a grab for the first available object, her fingers only finding the incense sticks. So she snatched one from its receptacle and held it out like a weapon. "Go away and leave me in peace, you demon!" she yelled, and slashed the air with the incense stick.

The ghostly little girl scowled at her. "You're one of them, aren't you?" she asked petulantly. "One of those horrible murderers who killed my family! Admit it, you old woman!" And to emphasize her words, she spat, aiming some kind of horrible green slime onto Emmanuella's nice oriental rug.

"I told you to go away!" replied Em. "I don't know who you are or what you want but you have to leave! This is *my* apartment and I want you gone!"

"No, this is my apartment," said the apparition angrily.

"No, this is my apartment," Em insisted.

"No, this is my apartment," the girl suddenly bellowed,

stomping her ghostly foot. And then she was upchucking a sort of green puke, spraying the vile, slimy, stinking substance all over the room, and on Em. And when she was all out of puke, the unwelcome visitor giggled unpleasantly, and abruptly withdrew into the wall next to the bookcase, leaving the entire room—and Emmanuella—dripping and smelling like raw sewage. The smelly kind.

The stuff was in Em's hair, on her face, soaking through her clothes, and then she was the one who was wailing and howling, for this was her best meditation and yoga outfit, and now it was totally and utterly ruined!

And even as she was spitting out the green gunk the monstrous visitor had showered her with, the door to the yoga room swung open, and the figure of a sturdily built young man appeared. He took one look at her and the room, and yelled out, "What the hell happened here, Mother?!"

"Oh, Darian! I've just been attacked… by a ghost!"

Chapter 2

Darian Watley wasn't used to seeing his mother like this. Usually she was dressed to the nines, her hair just so, her makeup immaculate, and her carriage making people think she was of royal descent. Not only was she looking like something a rat had dragged up from the London sewers, or dredged up from the bottom of the River Thames, but the entire room looked like a scene from *The Exorcist*, green slime covering the walls and furniture. Even the statuette of Buddha—one of his mother's treasures—was covered in the disgusting filth.

A tall man of imposing physique, nevertheless Darian felt a chill settle at the base of his spine. His mother, attacked in her own home? Unacceptable!

"What do you mean, a ghost?" he asked, his gray eyes searching around for the culprit. To his disappointment he saw no sign of him or her. For that a ghost was responsible was out of the question. He didn't believe in ghosts. Only the feeble-minded and the gullible did. Not Scotland Yard inspectors.

"Yes, a monstrous, filthy, horrible ghoul!"

"So where did he go?" He noticed that the window was closed shut, and the only other access to the room was the door he'd just come in through.

He'd heard his mother's screams through the wall dividing this room from his study in the apartment next door and had come running straightaway. He was used to hearing Em hum from time to time when she did her daily yoga and meditation routine, but now it had been as if all hell broke loose.

"It wasn't a he!" his mother now cried. "I'm telling you, Darian, it was a ghost. A small, female ghost..." She frowned, some goo dripping from her face. Green goo. "You know? Now that I come to think of it, she might have been a child. She was really small." She shook her head. "She said the most horrible things to me. Told me I was an old woman, Darian. Me! An old woman! How dare she! Oh, and she also said I was a murderer."

"A murderer?" he asked, surprised that his mother, usually the epitome of poise and calm, seemed so completely rattled now. "What do you mean?"

"Well, she said I'd murdered her family." She pressed her lips together and drew up her eyebrows in a display of censure. "What gall, to come in here and accuse me of murder in my own apartment. Oh, that's right. She kept saying this was *her* apartment. Oh, Darian, what am I going to do? How can I possibly meditate with a ghost lurking behind the bookcase?!"

At this, Darian directed a suspicious look at the bookcase, as if half expecting the prowler to pop up from behind it. "Where did you say you saw her?" he asked, inspecting the wall and the bookcase to a closer scrutiny.

"She was right where you're standing," she said, pointing in the direction of one of Deepak Chopra's more voluminous tomes. It was covered in the same gooey substance his mother was covered in, and smelled like the sewers of London. Not that he would know what the sewers of London would smell like because he'd never been down there, but he had a pretty good idea.

So he held his nose and eyed the wall critically, then shifted the bookcase. There was a lot of slime, but at first glance he could detect no sign of a strange little girl. There was also no evidence of a secret tunnel or an entrance, which was only logical, for since his study was on the other side of this wall, he would have noticed if some member of the London criminal classes had drilled a hole in the wall and used it to scare his mother witless.

"Nope," he finally concluded. "I got nothing. Are you sure she didn't escape through the window?"

"Of course I'm sure. I'm spooked but not insane." She was inspecting her wardrobe, and slapped her hand on her thigh. It made a squishy sound. "I think it's time to call in your friend, Darian. I'll bet she'll know what to do."

"My friend?" he asked, still searching around for a sign of the miscreant.

"Let's bring in Harry. If anyone can figure out what's going on it's her."

Alarmed, he looked up. "Oh, no," he said. "No, no, no. Not Harry again!"

But his mother directed a look of extreme censure at him. "Of course Harry. What do you have against her anyway? You know she's the best ghost hunter in London." She paused. "Well, she's probably the only ghost hunter in London. Hunting ghosts is kind of an emerging market I should think."

He shook his head adamantly. Ever since Harry had announced she was going to start her own ghost hunting business, he'd found it harder and harder to reconcile the warm feelings he harbored toward the young woman with the distaste he'd always felt toward the kind of charlatans who take advantage of people's gullibility to charge money to cleanse their homes from so-called ghosts and ghouls. It was a point of contention between them that had ended their brief relationship several weeks ago. Though his heart was still hers, and would always be, he knew, he simply couldn't accept this new line of work she'd engaged in, and most certainly not the fact that she insisted on carrying that idiot Jarrett Zephyr-Thornton as so much dead weight.

"I don't want you to call Harry, Mother," he said in measured tones. "You know I don't believe in all that nonsense and I certainly don't want you to encourage her," he quickly added before his mother could interrupt him.

"I know you don't believe in ghosts, Darian," she said primly, "but perhaps it's time you did, for your own mother has just been attacked by one, and I, for one, will not stand idly by while this monstrous... monster destroys my peace of mind and haunts and terrorizes me in my own home!"

And with these words she abruptly turned on her heel and strode out, making a sloshing sound as she did. He assumed she was going to take a long hot shower now, and put her yoga outfit in the washer.

And as he watched her stride out, he felt something churning in his gut. He hadn't seen Harry in weeks. Not since the row they had about her new business venture. And frankly he had no wish to see her again either. Not until she apologized and told him she was going to drop this ghost hunting nonsense. Stop making an utter and complete fool of herself.

He walked to the window and looked out, then checked it for signs of a break-in but found none. How this nasty piece of lowlife had gained access to the apartment was a mystery, but there had to be a perfectly reasonable explanation. No matter what his mother said, this was definitely not a ghost.

And he was just thinking about calling in his people to take a closer look when his mother returned, still covered in goo. She had her phone held delicately away from her ear, pinching it between manicured thumb and index finger and was speaking into it animatedly. "Yes, the ghost of a little girl, I'm sure of it now. She was projectile vomiting at me, Harry. Can you imagine?! Me!" Her voice quaked with a nice blend of indignation and sheer abhorrence. "And she absolutely ruined my yoga outfit and my yoga room!"

He wavered. Should he leave this matter to his mother or should he stay and try to figure out what was going on? It was obvious Em didn't need him here, but that didn't mean he had to go. Someone attacked her, and that someone was going to pay. So he decided to stick around. Deep down, he had to admit that his reasons for staying might have something to do with the imminent arrival of Harry McCabre, but he wasn't ready to admit that.

And when finally his mother disconnected and jubilantly announced, "She's coming! And she told me not to shower and not to touch anything!"

Darian groaned. "Oh, God," he muttered. "Is she bringing the idiot?"

His mother lifted her chin primly. "If you mean Jarrett, then yes, he's joining her. They're partners, remember? Where she goes, he goes. And I must say they're doing a really great job. Did you see the advertisement they placed in the Daily Mail? Very well done, I thought. Very professional."

He had seen it, and thought it was the most horrid thing. Ghost hunting. Bah! They called themselves the Wraith Wranglers now, and were funded by Jarrett's father, one of England's richest billionaires, or perhaps even the richest. And then of course Harry herself had had quite a windfall, when she'd inherited an antique store and a cool one million pounds from her former employer, the well-known antiquarian Sir Geoffrey Buckley.

He simply didn't understand how a nice, sensible, sweet-tempered young woman like Harry could ever engage in such a perfidious activity, but then again, it just went to show you never really knew a person, did you?

And as he stalked the apartment, anxiously awaiting Harry's arrival, he suddenly thought he heard a voice, but when he looked up, he saw nothing to indicate that there was anyone present apart from himself and his mother. But then the voice repeated, "Help. She's going to kill us! Help us, please!"

Chapter 3

Harry listened to the sound of the bells tinkling softly from her Amazon Echo and tried to will herself to sleep. Her snowy white Persian Snuggles was lying at her feet, her usual spot, her feet wrapped around her furry face, sleeping soundly and making soft snuffling sounds from time to time. Harry felt distinctly jealous that her feline roommate should find sleep so easily and didn't even need all the tricks she herself employed to battle her insomnia.

She was a petite young woman and didn't take up much space in the bed, which was a boon for Snuggles, as she liked to reserve ample space for herself, and Harry would have disturbed her peaceful slumber if she'd stretched the length of the bed. Harry's tousled blond hair now lay spread across the pillow, her pixie face screwed up in an expression of dismay when she realized sleep was a long time coming, as it had for the past few weeks.

She tossed and turned, sleep refusing to come, as it had since Buckley died and she'd inherited his store. She'd tried everything: herbal tea, face masks, hot baths, warm milk, and now this music which was supposed to make her sleep like a baby because it slowed down her brainwaves.

The effect on Harry was quite the opposite: her brainwaves seemed to be working overtime right now, as she couldn't stop thinking about the recent breakup with Darian, one of her favorite topics of contemplation lately.

She and the Scotland Yard inspector had gotten on so well, and she had to admit that her heart beat a little bit faster each time she heard his voice or saw his ruggedly handsome features. But then they'd had this terrible row over her idea to work as a ghost hunter and partner up with Jarrett, not one of Darian's favorite people. He didn't believe in ghosts, and was very vocal about it, expecting others to adhere to his view, which was so dictatorial!

It wasn't as if everyone believed the same thing. She believed in angels, for instance, and Darian didn't, but that didn't mean she couldn't, right? But he didn't see it that way: all intelligent people, a group in which he included her, had no right believing in such superstitious nonsense. And when she told him she believed the world was a flat disc carried on the backs of four elephants, standing on the back of a giant turtle called Great A'Tuin, he'd blown a gasket. Utter nonsense, he'd raged, even when she pointed out she was only joking, and sharing the joke with the late Sir Terry Pratchett.

He hadn't thought it was funny, and as she hadn't seen him since, probably still didn't. Well, whatever he thought, she was going ahead with her ghost helping business. Not that it mattered what he thought, as she would probably never see him again anyway, and nor did she want to.

She flipped onto her right side again and dug her head into the pillow with a groan. Snuggles snuffled, annoyed that her mistress wouldn't let her<> sleep in peace, and then, to add insult to injury, the phone rang. She snatched it up from the nightstand with a frown and saw it was Emmanuella. "Em?"

She listened patiently to Em's tale of ghostly woe, and instantly jumped from the bed, what little sleep there was now instantly wiped away.

"I'll be there in ten," she promised the woman, and then was on the phone with Jarrett, summoning her wraith wrangling counterpart.

A smile lit up her features as she patiently awaited the man's arrival. So she was going to see Darian again after all. She wondered what he thought about this ghostly apparition. He probably wasn't happy with it. Not just because his own mother had seen a ghost in her apartment, but because he was about to be confronted with a ghost of his own recent past as well. Two ghosts in one night. It was bound to rattle the unflappable Scotland Yard man, she reckoned, which was exactly what the pompous ass deserved.

Five minutes later, she got a call from Jarrett, announcing her chariot awaited, and she hurried down the stairs, excitement bubbling up inside her.

She didn't know why, but the thought suddenly occurred to her that this case might be the beginning of something new and beautiful. And even if it wasn't, she and Em and Jarrett would get to prove Darian Watley wrong.

Chapter 4

The ghostly phenomena they'd been studying had impressed Jarrett Zephyr-Thornton III greatly. That young, lanky billionaire's son had been a non-believer for most of his wastrel life, but had become a firm believer in only a matter of days when the recently deceased had started showing up en masse, upsetting the status quo of his placid and comfortable existence.

His was a regular and orderly life: in the morning his manservant Deshawn Little laid out his clothes for the day and served him breakfast at the Ritz-Carlton where he kept a suite year-round, and then he went about doing whatever took his fancy at that particular juncture in his life. It could be figure skating, or polo, or collecting rare and expensive Oldsmobiles. For with a father as rich as his, there was little reason to toil and slave away at a desk like most of his countrymen did, and he'd decided a long time ago that his life would consist of the pursuit of happiness only, a sacred mission he'd set himself and to which he'd adhered with rigid determination ever since.

"Step on it, Deshawn," he now said in his usual placid manner as the Rolls Royce Phantom tootled through London's congestion.

Even though the hour was late, and darkness had fallen hours before, traffic was still considerable. For London is the capital of the British Empire, that emerald island off the coast of Belgium, and therefore a city that never sleeps, not unlike Jarrett himself, who was a night owl and thought it wasteful not to use up as many hours in the day as God had provided, namely twenty-four.

He might not be gainfully employed, or even ungainfully, but that didn't stop him from making the most of the time he'd been given in this world.

His most recent hobby was helping ghosts move on to the afterlife and convince them not to bother the living. It was a noble quest, and one in which he'd found the perfect partner in Harry McCabre. She was great with ghosts, whereas he was great with Harry, which made theirs a well-oiled team.

It had come as a pleasant surprise to hear that this latest trifle of trouble had occurred at Em's, one of his favorite people in the world. Even though she'd produced a Scotland Yard man for a son, which happens to the best of us and wasn't something he held against her, she was a dear, dear friend.

It would be fun to see Darian again, who lately had decided to tear himself away from their small and merry band, due to some irreconcilable differences between himself and Harry. Darian didn't believe in ghosts, for some reason, and Harry did, which explained the whole trouble in a nutshell.

Finally, they arrived at Valentine Street number nine, and he opened the door to let Harry in. He liked to travel in style, and since Harry refused to buy herself a decent automobile but instead insisted on bicycling herself around London, he'd kindly offered the use of his Rolls as the official transportation mode for the Wraith Wranglers. It was not because they were ghost helpers and as such the object of much ridicule that they had to lower themselves even more by using public transportation, he felt.

"So Em is having some ghost trouble, is she?" he asked, settling back against the fawn leather seats once more and steepling his fingers. His fair hair was brushed back from his noble brow, his Tom Ford costume immaculate, and for the occasion he was wearing his favorite tawny brogues.

Harry, dressed in ripped jeans and a gray hoodie as usual, grinned from ear to ear. "You don't have to rub it in, Jarrett."

He arched an eyebrow. "Rub what in?" he asked innocently.

"Darian. He's going to be livid that his mother decided to call us in."

"Oh, but I hadn't even thought of that," he said quite insincerely.

"I'll bet you hadn't," she muttered, and glanced out the window.

He gave her a scrutinizing look. She looked very pale, as she had for the past few weeks, a fact which didn't fail to worry. He now said as much in as delicate a way as possible. "You look like hell, Harry. Positively ghastly."

She lifted her hands ineffectually. "I don't sleep! I just don't. I go to bed when it's time to go, but I simply lie awake all night, and in the morning I get up because… well, because it's time to get up and I've got stuff to do."

"Mh. Insomnia. Yes, that is a nuisance," he agreed. Though he himself had never suffered from the debilitating affliction, he could see how annoying it would be. "Have you tried—"

She held up a hand. "Let me stop you right there. Trust me, I've tried everything. "Herbal tea, warm milk, alpha wave music, even one of those cherry pit pillows—the ones you heat up in the microwave? Nothing works!"

"I was going to say pills," he now said. "Have you tried sleeping pills?"

"No pills!" she stated adamantly, as he'd known she would. Harry was one of those strictly healthy people, who dreamed of growing their own veggies, subsisting on a strict vegetarian diet of organic food, and adhering to alternative medicine only, taking a dim view of the pharmaceutical industry.

It was a stance he couldn't help but admire, like one vaguely admires practitioners of BDSM for their love of suffering and pain. Certain religious leaders would have loved her, for they, too, were great admirers of hardship.

"Well, if you change your mind my doctor once prescribed me some excellent sleeping tablets. Not that I need them, for I sleep like a baby—or, to stay within the evening's theme, like the dead." Perhaps he shouldn't have mentioned what a sound sleeper he was, for it was rubbing it in a bit, but Harry wasn't going to listen to his advice anyway, as her next words proved.

"No pills. Sooner or later my body will return to its normal pattern. I just have to stick it out." She mused for a moment. "Perhaps it's the Wi-Fi?"

"The what?" he asked, though he knew perfectly well what she meant.

"There are a lot of Wi-Fi signals in the building," she explained. "I'm sure all that radiation can't be good for the human body. Perhaps I should build myself one of those Faraday cages to keep out electromagnetic radiation?"

"Or you could wear lead pajamas and a tinfoil nightcap," he suggested.

She eyed him curiously. "You know, that's not such a bad idea. Do you think they exist?"

But his mind had already taken possession of the image and was running with it. "Do you think Faraday cages keep out ghosts as well? If so, we could have them mass-produced in China and then sell them over here. Establish our Wraith Wrangling franchise on a firmer financial footing."

"Maybe," she admitted. "But I doubt many people like to sleep in a cage."

"Myes, I see your point. The only one who would like the idea is our mutual friend Darian Watley, but then again he's in the cage business."

The mention of the man's name seemed to annoy Harry, for she suddenly frowned and said, "I think we should focus on our services for now, Jarrett."

And she was right, of course. In the short span of time they'd offered their ghost helping services, they'd become something of a minor phenom, being summoned on a daily basis to deal with this ghostly problem or that annoying wraith. Still he felt they could do more. At heart he was the son of an entrepreneur and he now saw a lot of potential for merchandising. They could become a one-stop shop for everything spooky, and sell to the unsuspecting public any number of devices to keep baying ghosts at bay.

"Let's just keep it simple for now," suggested Harry. "I don't want us to become a joke, Jarrett. We're just here to communicate with the dead, not to scare the living daylights out of them with all kinds of devices or tricks."

"Scaring the living daylights out of the living is the business of the dead, so scaring the living daylights out of them seems like a fair way of returning the favor," he pointed out.

"And that's where you're wrong," she said sternly. "We are here to *help* ghosts, not to scare them. They're lost spirits, not ghouls or monsters."

"And that's where we differ," he said softly, and glanced over. Once more he thought he detected in her a distinct lack of the good old jolliness with which the old Harry McCabre had been imbued. She'd become far too serious for his taste, and seemed to be determined to take the fun out of this entire wraith wrangling enterprise.

The only reason he'd agreed to join the endeavor was because it promised to be a hoot, but now with Harry seeming to feel they were on a sacred quest to help wraiths, frankly he was starting to feel bored with the whole setup. He had any number of other endeavors he could grace with his time, good name and fortune, and he was running out of reasons why he shouldn't.

"Look, it's not as if we're doing this out of the goodness of our hearts, Harry," he now said perhaps a little more acidly than he'd intended. "At its core this is a business enterprise and that's the way it should be managed."

She looked up as if stung. "A business enterprise? Is that how you see it?"

"Of course. Why else do anything if not to turn a big, fat profit?"

Her face took on a crimson hue now, a distinct improvement from the pale pallor it had presented before, though he wasn't sure it was for the best. "Look, I'm doing this simply because I want to help lost spirits, not to monetize them!" she said heatedly. "Which is why I suggested we charge an absolute minimum for our services. This is a public service, not business."

"I'm afraid we don't see eye to eye then, Harry, for I, for one, feel we should charge a pretty penny for a service as unique and in demand as ours."

Her eyes were blazing now, and he shuffled uncomfortably in his seat. Harry was a little scary when she got mad. "You want out, is that it?"

"No, of course not. I just want—"

"I knew it!" she cried. "I knew you weren't going to see this through!"

Denying the foul charge vehemently, he said, "You have to admit that lately you haven't been much fun to be around, Harry. Your gloomy goosery has reached a point that it's become almost unbearable! It has started to affect me unfavorably. Yesterday I had my first fit of depression in years!"

"Oh, and that's my fault, is it?"

"Well..."

"You know?" she asked, narrowing her eyes, "if you want out, I'll give you your out right now, Jarrett Zephyr-Thornton the Third. That way you'll never have to stand my gloomy goosery again and you can go on living your happy, happy life!" And then she bellowed, "Deshawn, stop the car!"

Deshawn, always the picture of helpfulness, did as he was told, and before Jarrett could respond, she had opened the door and was crawling out of the Rolls. "Um. What are you doing?" he asked now.

"Bye bye, Jarrett. Have a great life!" she snapped, then slammed the door in his face with quite a bit more vim and vigor either Mr. Rolls or Mr. Royce had ever designed their vehicle to withstand.

And then she was off at a brisk pace. He stared after her disappearing back for a moment, and felt an unfamiliar pang of sorrow. Why he felt this pang, he didn't know, for he'd never felt it before. But he didn't like it.

Chapter 5

Harry trudged on. It appeared there weren't that many cabs around at this late hour, or at least not in the part of the city where Deshawn had dropped her off. She felt tears sting behind her eyes as she thought of the recent spat. It was so unfair of Jarrett to consider the undertaking they'd started as a business and nothing more. Helping ghosts wasn't merely a business. It was a mission. A calling. A genuine vocation. But then what did she expect? Jarrett was the son of a billionaire and one of the richest men in the country. To him probably everything was a business, even helping ghosts.

And as she walked on, she was aware of a keen sense of betrayal. She'd known going in that there was always a risk he might get bored with the Wraith Wranglers—or her—but now that it had happened she felt miserable she'd been right. She'd hoped the Wraith Wranglers would prove the one project he gave his all, and that their friendship as well as their partnership would last. Jarrett was eccentric, but in a fun way, and she loved him.

So she'd become a gloomy goose, huh? Well, perhaps he was right. He'd told her before that she was taking this ghost thing far too seriously, and blamed her bad mood on Darian, who'd 'spoiled' her. She knew that wasn't it. Something had happened to make her become introspective. Less exuberant than before. And it had all begun when Sir Geoffrey Buckley had left her the store and that money. Somehow it had made her feel she had a responsibility now. Toward him and his faith in her. She needed to return the favor somehow and show the world that she was worthy of this great gift. And somewhere along the way she'd lost herself. A little. Or maybe a lot.

She walked on. Em's house wasn't much further. She could reach it on foot without much effort. So she took out her phone and told Em that she was running a little late. She also told her she would arrive as a party of one, having left her sidekick by the wayside.

"What?" cried Em. "But why? Did you two have a fight?"

Tears once again stung behind her eyes. "He told me I'm a gloomy goose," she lamented. "And he thinks I'm too soft on the ghosts, Em, and he wants to make money from them, too." Even as she said the words, they sounded silly to her ears, nothing a good, long talk between friends couldn't clear up. But she didn't feel like having a good, long talk with Jarrett, or any talk at all.

"Oh, honey," said Em, her soft voice soothing. "Don't you worry about Jarrett. I'm sure he'll be back."

"I don't want him to be back," she said adamantly. "Besides, I'll bet he's got a hundred other projects already lined up to replace this one. He was always only half on board with this, Em. Never completely committed. I'll bet he's halfway to the Caribbean by now, to see if this Bermuda Triangle thing is real or not. Or maybe he's going to compete on *The Voice* and become the next Blake Shelton!" Her voice was trailing off as she broke down in sobs.

"Why don't you give him a few days to cool off and then call him?"

She shook herself and decided that this was nonsense. "I'm sorry, Em. This is not about Jarrett or me. This is about your encounter with a ghost."

"Oh, that little thing," said Em. "That ghost is long gone, honey, though Darian insists he's hearing voices now."

This took her aback. "Darian is hearing voices?"

"Yes, can you imagine? It's got him pretty shook up."

"I'm going to take care of this for you, Em," she promised. "I'm going to make your apartment ghost-free, all right?" And she was already steeling herself for the upcoming task. Jarrett might think working with ghosts was boring, but she knew for a fact that it wasn't. That it was a noble quest that she pursued with the same dedication she applied to everything in life.

When she finally arrived, Em was waiting for her in the small vestibule of her apartment building, and as they rode the elevator up together, she said, "Darian isn't very happy about this, Harry, but don't let that stop you, all right? You just do what you have to do and don't mind my imbecile son."

"I'll try to ignore him," she promised.

Em glanced at her up and down, and said, "I would have thought you ghostbusting types were carrying a ton of equipment and special suits?"

She laughed. "That's in the movies, Em. In real life things are a lot less complicated. I just want to talk to this specter. See what I can find out about her. Usually all they want is attention and someone to guide them. They're often confused souls who need direction, that's all. No gadgets are necessary to provide them with a little kind-hearted help," she assured Em with a smile.

She noticed her hostess wasn't dressed to the nines as usual. Instead, she was wearing a yoga outfit that was covered top to bottom in dried-up green muck, as if she'd been cavorting in a ditch somewhere. The stuff was even on her face and in her hair. "Why didn't you take a shower?" she asked now.

"Take a shower? You told me not to!" Em cried.

"Oh, that's right. I forget." She scooped up a generous helping of goo and examined it closely. "Just your regular ectoplasmic residue," she pointed out. "Nothing to worry about. And I'll bet it's even good for your complexion."

"It is? You mean like a face mask?"

"Yup. Exactly like a face mask."

"Oh, I must scrape it off and reuse it. My friends are going to be so jealous when I tell them! I'll bet even Gwyneth Paltrow has never heard of ghost ectoplasm as a face mask!" Then she frowned thoughtfully. "Do you think we could commercialize this? Bottle it up and slap a label on it? There's big money in anti-aging and anti-wrinkle creams, Harry. Big, big money."

Harry sighed. "You sound just like Jarrett. He wants us to start merchandising the Wraith Wranglers. Sell Faraday cages and all kinds of junk to 'protect' people from ghosts. I told him exactly what I thought about that."

"You don't want to make money?" Em guessed.

Her face set, she declared, "Absolutely not. For me this is a holy quest, Em. I want to help these unfortunate souls to move on, not use them to make a quick buck. We're in the business of helping people, not exploiting them!"

"Jarrett's in the doghouse, huh?" asked Em with a funny look on her face.

"He's bored. He wants to move onto the next big project already. He's done this for a few weeks and that's about as far as he's willing to go. The man's got the attention span of a gnat, Em, so this was to be expected."

They arrived with a soft bump and got off. And then she saw

that Darian was waiting for her, and a shock galvanized her system. He always had this effect on her. His sturdy frame, his anvil jaw, his remarkably perceptive gray eyes... They all served to make her spine turn to jelly and her stomach to make a double backflip and tie itself into a complicated macramé.

"Hello, Darian," she said in what she hoped was a cool, detached voice.

"Hello, Harry," he returned, his face revealing nothing. Whether he was glad to see her or not was impossible to determine. So she quickly moved past him and into Em's cozy apartment without another word. She was here to do a job, not to engage Darian Watley in conversation.

She set a course for the meditation room, where the drama had played out. She knew her way around Em's apartment, having stayed there before.

The meditation room was covered top to bottom with the same green gunk Em was covered with, and she eyed it reverently. "Oh, my," she whispered. This was one angry spirit. To display so much annoyance something must be bugging her a great deal indeed.

"Where did you say you saw her?" she asked.

Em pointed at the bookcase, which was moved a few inches away from the wall. "Right there. Darian looked but he saw nothing out of the ordinary."

She knelt down next to the spot Em indicated and closed her eyes, trying to get a sense of this being. But nothing came to her. Nothing even registered on her spook radar, which was more sensitive than most people's.

"I've checked the entire room," now Darian's stentorian voice sounded, and a distinct tingle crept up Harry's neck. He still had that power over her.

"Please just let me do my job, Darian," she said. "And be quiet."

"You're wasting your time," he insisted. "There's nothing here."

"Em said you heard a voice?" she asked, giving him a stern look.

He hesitated. "I did hear… something," he admitted.

"What did the voice say?"

He shrugged. "Probably just my imagination."

"What did it say?" she insisted.

"Please help us. They're going to kill my little brother."

Chapter 6

They'd been driving around aimlessly after Harry had left, and Deshawn now asked whether Jarrett wished to return to the Ritz Carlton. He frowned, and subjected his conscience to a thorough examination. No, he didn't want to return to the Ritz just yet. If he was absolutely honest with himself he wanted to join Harry on this latest quest. Why they'd suddenly parted on such harsh terms he didn't know. One minute he was suggesting they expand the business and the next their partnership was at a rather abrupt end.

So when finally the car pulled to a stop and he glanced out the window, he saw that Deshawn had parked the Rolls across the street from Em's place.

"What are we doing here, Deshawn?" he asked his loyal servant.

"I thought you might have had a change of heart, sir," said the man.

Deshawn was a thickset man, with a thinning mane of hair, and had been Jarrett's second-in-command for so long now he was more a friend than a servant. He wouldn't know what to do without him, to be absolutely honest.

"A change of heart, eh? And you encourage such a phenomenon?"

"I feel this wraith wrangling endeavor has quite a bit of merit, sir."

"Merit? Please elucidate, Deshawn."

Deshawn turned around in his seat so he could address his employer directly. "This is the first time I've seen you this enthusiastic about a specific project, sir. And it is, if you pardon my presumptuousness, quite refreshing."

"What? That's not true. I liked the space shuttle program, remember?"

"Hardly, sir. You were merely going through the motions."

"Or what about when I was going to become England's next rock star?"

"You lacked both the wherewithal and the conviction, sir."

"Or the figure skating? I could have been a bloody good figure skater."

"Your enthusiasm was tepid, sir, as was your grip on the ice. Merely a means to fill up an emptiness at the heart of your life, if I may be so bold, sir."

"You may be so bold, Deshawn," he muttered thoughtfully. "So you really think this ghost thing is the bee's knees, eh? The whole ball of wax?"

"It provides you with the opportunity to make a difference in the world."

"Hogwash. I've never wanted to make a difference in the world, Deshawn. You know I don't believe in that kind of nonsense. I'm a cynical, practical man, not Mother Teresa or Angelina Jolie."

"Quite, sir. But indubitably wrangling wraiths offers one a certain satisfaction when guiding these poor lost souls onto the right track."

"It does give one a certain gratification, doesn't it?" he asked, musing about this extraordinary aspect of the matter. It was so unlike him, he meant to say, to care about other human beings, even though they were quite dead, of course.

"It has worked a great change in you, sir."

He crooked an eyebrow. "A change for the better or the worse?"

"Definitely for the better, sir," Deshawn said with the tremor of a smile.

"Very well. I must admit the venture has brought me considerable pleasure, but it irks me that Harry seems adamant to take it into an almost religious direction. The holy fire burns brightly in that one, Deshawn."

"That's merely because she has an ulterior motive, sir," opined Deshawn. "Even though she may not even be aware of it herself."

"Ulterior motive, eh? And what might this ulterior motive be?"

Deshawn gave him an indulgent smile. "You know her motivation, sir."

"Oh, right. You mean the parent thing?"

"Indeed, sir. The death of one's parents at such a young age is a very powerful motivator."

"Yes, I see what you mean. So she's still hoping to get into contact with her deceased mater and pater, mh?"

"That is the interpretation I put upon the matter, sir. It would explain the solemnity with which she's pursuing her wraith wrangling endeavor."

"Very well, then. And you feel I should lend her a helping hand?"

"Yes, sir. It will make you a better man."

He burst into a pleasant laugh at this. "A better man. My God,

Deshawn. Now you're starting to worry me. Don't tell me you've taken up religion."

Over Deshawn's face had stolen a look of solemnity that wouldn't have been out of place on Harry's features. "Not at all. At one point we all need to decide on our purpose in life and come to terms with the choices we make."

He eyed the man curiously. "You're quite the philosopher, Deshawn."

"Thank you, sir. If I may venture a guess, that might be part of my particular purpose in life."

"And mine is to help Harry get in touch with her folks, eh?"

"Yes, sir," said Deshawn with pretty humility and candor.

"If you say so. I don't see why not. I mean, it's not as if I've got something else to occupy my time at this particular juncture." And with these noble words, which would have made both Mother Teresa and Angelina Jolie swell with pretty pride, he jauntily exited the car and strolled across the street to aid and abet Harry in this latest ghost helping adventure of hers.

He might not be as quixotic and self-sacrificing as Harry, but Deshawn had a point. For some reason helping ghosts made him feel good about himself, and since he was a hedonist at heart, feeling good was good enough for him. And then of course there was the fact that his mere presence would annoy the hell out of one Inspector Darian Watley of Scotland Yard. It was small gifts like these that brought the sunshine into one's life, he felt.

Deshawn, falling into step next to him, muttered softly, "If I may say so, sir, I think you're to be commended for taking the high road."

"Well, what other road is there for us billionaires, Deshawn?"

"Touché, sir."

Chapter 7

There was a loud growling noise, a snarl as if from some wild animal, and Bruna Mars paused her ironing, listening intently. The TV was playing in the living room but not that loud, unless Ella had turned the sound up, as she sometimes did when there was a show on that she liked. Her iron poised over the work shirt she was ironing, she waited and listened, but when there was no repetition of the sound, she resumed her work.

A big woman with an abundance of curly hair that framed a heart-shaped face, she was soon lost once again in thought, staring out the window of the small office that doubled as a washroom. Outside a drizzle was lashing London. She shook her head and tsk-tsked. It was one of those days when the sun refused to shine and the British capital seemed cloaked in darkness for days on end, sometimes stretching into weeks. The weather affected her mood, though she tried not to let it.

She placed the ironed shirt on the pile and glimpsed at the poster of some tropical destination she'd tacked up on the wall. Some food for her dreams of one day leaving London and its nasty weather behind and moving to more sunny climes. Mh-mh. She could live near a white sandy beach like that, she thought, and drink from coconuts and swim in the pristine waters.

Ella interrupted her thoughts by stating in a slow, halting voice, "Mummy? The monster wants me to feed it. So... can I?"

"Sure, honey," she said without looking up. "What does the monster want?"

"Well, it says it wants meat. It says it hasn't eaten meat in a very long time and it misses the taste of the iron in the blood."

This bugged her, so she turned, her hand on her hip. "Have you been watching shows for grownups again? You know you can't switch channels."

"No, Mummy," said Ella, the cutest five-year-old in the world and the most precocious one. She just loved to watch National Geographic or the Discovery Channel. "It's just that... the monster says... that if I don't give him meat... he's going to eat me! So I has to feed him! Maybe a sausage?"

Bruna smiled at this. Such a vivid imagination. It was just incredible that a five-year-old could be playing these kinds of games already.

"Eat you, huh? Now why would any monster want to eat you I just can't understand." She knelt down and picked up her kid, then tickled her. "Is it perhaps because you're so cute, huh? Could that be the reason?"

Ella laughed loudly at this. "Mummy! You're tickling me!"

"Sometimes I want to eat you!" she said, holding her upside down and carrying her into the living room. The TV was still blaring and some cartoon monsters were chasing one another. So she plunked her little girl down on the couch. "Now just watch the show, hon, and don't worry about feeding the monsters. They're not real, see? They're just cartoons inside the television."

Ella looked up at her with a questioning look in her big chocolate eyes. "But this monster wasn't on the TV, Mummy.

This one was in the kitchen, making a real mess!"

She laughed again. "Sure it was, honey. Are you sure that the monster in the kitchen wasn't you? Huh? Are you hungry?"

"I'm not hungry," she said seriously. "But the monster is. Maybe *you* can feed it? Because I don't know where the meat is," she concluded, holding up her hands, palms upward.

She was just the most adorable girl in the world, Bruna thought not for the first time, and instantly the twin thought came on the heels of the first one that Muhammed didn't know what he was missing after walking out on them.

"So you want meat now, huh?" she asked, and was just about to switch channels to something less monstrous, when that same noise sounded again, snarling and growling. She frowned, for this time it was obvious that it wasn't coming from the TV at all. It sounded more like it came from… the kitchen.

With a questioning look at Ella, who now gave the cutest shrug, as if to say, 'See? I told you so!' she slowly walked toward the kitchen. But then she was held back by Ella's voice, as she implored, "Be careful, Mummy. The monster is very big and ugly and if you're not careful it will eat you alive!"

She held up a hand to silence her daughter, then picked up the baseball bat she always kept handy next to the front door, in case her ex-husband with one of his drunk buddies showed up, and took a firm grip on the handle with two hands. She proceeded into the kitchen, following the snarls and snorts as she prepared herself to take a good swing at whoever had the gall to enter her apartment and scare her and her little girl half to death by demanding food.

She was a big woman, but she moved with grace and poise and surprising agility. And then she pounced on the intruder, and her jaw dropped. It wasn't Muhammed at all. In the middle of the kitchen, right in front of the fridge, a spreading old man was sitting squarely on the floor, scooping up food from the fridge and depositing it into his mouth, snarling and snorting loudly as he did so. When she surprised him he was just making short shrift of a casserole of lamb chops, grease dripping from his lips.

His face was bloated and had a greenish mottled tinge, his eyes dark-rimmed and milky, and his hair matted to a pale skull. But the worst part of all was his fat belly, which was slit open, and the food he was stuffing into his face was simply falling through him and onto the floor, making a mess.

And then she was screaming, and dropped the baseball bat when the old man snarled, "I want meat, woman! Give me meat! Bloody, juicy meat!"

Chapter 8

Not far from where Bruna was screaming her head off, Mörten Horrocks was preparing his speech in front of the mirror. He was the newly appointed conductor of the London Symphonic Orchestra and had just been accepted for another three years as its principal conductor due to the fine work he'd done with the orchestra. Tonight he was going to give his acceptance speech and thank the members of the orchestra for their unwavering support and the excellence of their work. For the occasion he was dressed up to the nines, in his best tuxedo, complete with cummerbund and silk tie.

First they'd give a nice rendition of a part of Beethoven's Missa Solemnis, and then there would be a reception for patrons and sponsors where his appointment would be officially announced. Mörten, a spindly man originally hailing from Sweden, had followed the opportunities where they arose, and eventually those opportunities had brought him to the British capital.

"Dear members of the board, dear esteemed members of the orchestra, and of course, last but not least, dear members of the audience," he muttered while fiddling with his tie. As a rule, he never wore ties, for they made him feel as if he were about to be hanged by the neck until death ensued.

"Honey!" the voice of his wife came from the en-suite bathroom, "do you think I should go for the Vera Wang or wear something more formal?"

"As formal as possible!" he yelled back.

"Are you sure? I talked to Rupert's wife last week and she said she was going to make sure to display quite a bit of cleavage!"

"No cleavage! The members of the board are all very conservative elderly gentleman. They don't want cleavage, they want prim and proper, honey!"

Tamatha, his wife of three years, now popped her tousled head from the bathroom, where she was currently in the process of making herself look so splendid she would undoubtedly steal his thunder at the reception. Not that he minded. She was a gorgeously beautiful woman and he loved looking at her quite a bit himself.

They'd met when he was a guest conductor at the Okinawa Philharmonic Orchestra. She was one of the orchestra's bassoon players, and throughout the first rehearsal she'd caught his eye—and his ear—and they'd kept eye contact throughout. Afterward, they'd met for coffee and pretty soon the wedding bells of the local church had rung out a blithe peal, easily the best day of his life, and the best thing that had ever happened to him, bar none.

"You better don't give them a heart attack," he warned. "They still have to sign my contract."

She giggled, a perfect row of white teeth showing. "What about my contract, huh? They still haven't approved my residency."

"After tonight they will," he said confidently. Now that he was the official conductor of one of London's most prestigious symphonic orchestras, the world was pretty much his oyster.

"Dear members of the board," he began again when Tamatha's

head retreated into the bathroom once again, but halted when he heard a soft sniffling sound. "Honey?" he asked. "Are you all right?"

"Sure," her voice came back. "Just trying to figure out which dress to wear."

He paused the fidgeting with his tie for a moment, listening intently. Yes. There it was again. A soft sniffle, as if from a child crying softly in a corner. His eyes strayed to the corner, which held Tamatha's rehearsal setup: her bassoon on its stand, the lectern with the music score and her chair. Then, as he squinted, he thought he saw the vague outline of... a child, right behind the big, bulky silver suitcase Tamatha used to carry her bassoon around.

His heart skipped a beat. He was a very practical man, and not a believer in the supernatural at all, but he was wondering... if this was a ghost.

He approached the wispy figure warily, then crouched down next to it. Yes, now he could see her clearly, her face pale as the moon, her eyes black as coal, and a body so wispy it was like a bank of fog on the Scottish moors.

"Hey," he said softly. "Hey, little girl. What's the matter? Are you lost?"

The little girl looked up at this, as if surprised that anyone would pay attention to her. Then she raised both arms and reached out to him as if to say, 'Please, pick me up.' And he was just about to lift her from behind Tamatha's chair when suddenly a dark frown appeared on her small brow and her face opened up into a wide maw, and then she was chucking a long stream of green slime at him!

And even as he fell back, arms and legs flailing like an upturned beetle, she was covering his nice new tux and his nice new silk tie, and pretty much the rest of him as well, in a relentless stream of thick, gooey green slime. And then he collapsed onto his back on the floor, sputtering and screaming.

When Tamatha came rushing in, drawn by the noise, and saw her husband lying on the floor, covered in muck, she raised her hands to her face, and cried, "Mörten! Wha—what happened?!" And when he told her there was a very unpleasant little girl in the corner, upchucking on her bassoon, she directed a gaze there, but all she said was, "There's nothing there, honey."

And when he'd removed a good portion of green gunk from his face and opened his eyes, he saw she was right: the corner was empty! He shook his head in extreme dismay. "We need to call those people, Tamatha! We need to call those Wraith Wranglers! I swear to God! This apartment is haunted!"

"All right, all right," she said, and with shaking fingers took out her cell and hurried over to snatch up the copy of the latest Daily Mail. She quickly flipped through its pages to the classifieds and found the advertisement Mörten had circled with red ballpoint pen. He'd meant it as a joke, to give to one of his colleagues in the orchestra, but now it seemed bitter reality.

She quickly scanned the advertisement. It read, 'Are you suffering from the insufferable company of wraiths? Are they haunting your home and hearth? Are they making your life an unliving and unlivable hell? Fear not! Wraith Wranglers to the rescue! These fearless spook stalkers are on the job! At your ghost-battling service twenty-four-seven. Call in Harry and Jarrett, London's very own Wraithbusters.'

Chapter 9

Darian watched the proceedings with a kindling eye. Not only did he think the whole thing was simply some kind of practical joke someone was playing on his mother, he thought Harry was exacerbating the situation by feeding her irrational belief in ghosts. There was nothing out of the ordinary except someone playing a trick. All he needed to do was bring in his team so they could expose the prankster.

Only trouble was, he didn't want to saddle his people up with such a silly assignment, as they had real crimes to solve. They didn't need to waste their time by hunting a practical jokester. And then there was his mother's wish that Harry take care of this. A desire he better not thwart lest he wanted to start open warfare between himself and his obstinate, superstitious mum.

"What do you hope to find?" he asked acerbically. "A troll hiding behind the bookcase? A three-legged ghoul? It's probably just a practical joke."

Without facing him, Harry asked, "Then where did all that green stuff come from? Explain me that."

"I don't know, but I'm sure there's a perfectly rational explanation."

She rose and wiped her hands on her jeans. "Like what? There's nothing here. No pipes, no sprinkler system, no evidence of tampering whatsoever."

He had to admit she had a point. He himself had found nothing out of the ordinary either. Still, there simply had to be something. But before he could expound his theory, the doorbell rang and Em said, "That'll be Jarrett."

Both he and Harry looked up at this, Harry with a look of surprise and he with one of supreme loathing. "Oh, God," he groaned. "Not that idiot, too."

But then Jarrett strode in, looking the picture of the aristocratic overlord visiting the modest hovel of one of his vassals, and said with a supercilious look on his face, "Darian, I hadn't expected to find you here. Hello, Harry."

"Jarrett," she acknowledged with an odd gleam in her eye. "What are you doing here?"

"Oh, I just happened to be in the neighborhood, so I thought I'd drop in. Have you found the source of the upheaval?" he asked, kneeling down and subjecting the wall to a fierce scrutiny.

"I thought you weren't going to do this anymore!" she hissed, which gave Darian the impression that not all was well in the wraith wrangling Garden of Eden, and that a snake in the grass had muddled relations between these two.

"I changed my mind," he said. "Ours is a lofty goal, Harry, and the foul stench of the baser type of commerce has no business there. I see that now."

"Did you figure that out all by yourself?" she asked, but then another person entered the room, and they all looked up. It was Deshawn Little, Jarrett's inseparable sidekick, and Darian groaned even more. This place was starting to resemble a gathering of fools, and he, for once, was starting to feel awfully out of place. Nevertheless he refused to leave. This was his mother's apartment and he had a right to be here just as much as this bunch of morons.

"I pointed out to Mr. Zephyr-Thornton that ours is a noble quest," Deshawn now piped up, and Harry gave him a beaming smile, "and he decided to give it his all from now on. Isn't that a correct synopsis, sir?"

"Well put as usual, Deshawn. In layman's terms, I was wrong and you were right, Harry." He eyed her contritely, a look that quite clearly didn't come naturally to him, for he squinted terribly. "Forgive me, pretty please?"

To Darian's horror, she slung her arms around him and kissed him on the lips. "Of course I forgive you, you big doofus!" she cried happily. "But only if you promise me not to go all Jack Welch on me again, you hear?"

"I solemnly swear I won't," he declared, his fingers in the air.

"Besides, it's not as if you need the money," she pointed out. "In fact this can be your way of atoning for robbing the British population blind."

"There was never any robbing involved in the creation of the Zephyr-Thornton fortune," he declared. "Everything was perfectly aboveboard."

"Right," she said dubiously. "Just hard work and industriousness."

"That's exactly right. Our little nest egg was built the legal and correct way, and no animals or small children were harmed in the obtaining of it."

Darian, who became aware that Deshawn had sidled up to him, glanced over. "What do you want?" he snapped, doing little to conceal his distaste.

"Merely to inquire whether you have determined the source

of the upheaval, Inspector," Deshawn inquired in his usual mellifluous voice.

Darian tilted his chin defiantly. "I have not. Because my mother insists on bringing in a bunch of quacks to deal with what I'm sure is a simple hoax."

"I see," said Deshawn deferentially. "Would it perhaps satisfy you to know that two more incidents have occurred within the last hour? And that they both took place in units contained within this very same complex?"

"What?!" cried Darian, and Harry, too, expressed her surprise.

Deshawn took out his phone and read the coordinates of one Mörten Horrocks and one Bruna Mars, who'd called the Wraith Wranglers hotline.

"But those are our neighbors!" cried Darian.

"They've asked us to pay them a visit, as they're being troubled by the presence of some very nasty wraiths. If I'm not mistaken, ectoplasm was involved, just as it was with Mrs. Sheetenhelm's unwanted visitor."

Em, who now strode in, looking fresh-faced after a shower, asked, "What's going on? What's with all the excitement?"

"There are two more cases of muck-spraying ghouls," said Harry, giving a succinct summary of the situation. "And they're your neighbors."

When Deshawn gave her the names, she said, "That's odd. Some people were murdered in those apartments, weren't they, Darian? A long time ago?"

Chapter 10

The news shook Harry. "Murders?" she asked. "Here?"

"Don't you remember, Darian? Bruna Mars told me the story. Said it was such a coincidence that two apartments would have the scenes of a murder in the same building." She'd lifted her hands to her face, inspecting the effects of the green goo. She seemed less affected by this terrible news than the rest of the gathering, who all stood eyeing her with horror etched on their faces. All except Darian, who, like his mother, appeared remarkably unperturbed.

"What about this apartment? Were there any murders here?" Jarrett asked. He'd stepped away from the wall, in case the girl reappeared.

Em shook her head. "No way. I specifically asked Broderick and he assured me this apartment was never the scene of any ghastly business. He knew that I would never have taken it if it had. Isn't that right, Darian?"

But Darian continued mysterious, refusing to confirm or deny. Harry half expected him to hold up his hand and bark a strict, "No comment!"

"So since the murders took place in a different part of the

building that was fine by me," Em said. "I mean, this is London, Harry. Every family has its cross to bear. Going straight back to those pesky Romans and Londinium the place must be literally littered with corpses. We were simply lucky that no murder ever took place in here." She shivered. "I wouldn't be able to live in an apartment where someone was murdered, would you?"

Harry eyed her keenly now. "Em, a murder *did* take place here." She pointed at the bookcase. "Where else do you think the girl came from?" She turned to Jarrett. "We better go over to the other apartments to have a look."

He nodded solemnly. "We'd better," he agreed.

Em's eyes had widened to their widest possible dilation. "Murder? In my apartment? In my meditation space? But that's not possible!" She turned to her son. "Darian! Tell me it's not true. Tell me my sacred space is unspoiled."

But the dignified silence he assumed spoke volumes.

Her hands flew to her face again, this time not to check on the anti-aging effect of ectoplasm but to check if the top of her head hadn't popped off at this terrible news. "I've been meditating in this room for months! And doing yoga! Right here, where a child was brutally slain!" Then she narrowed her eyes. "What else didn't you tell me, you inconsiderate brute?!"

"There's no need for all the drama," he grumbled. "It's not because a few murders happened in this building that it's suddenly a health hazard."

"But why didn't you or your father tell me?!" she demanded

"Because of this! We knew you'd overreact and make a big deal of it."

Her voice shook with righteous indignation, and Harry felt for her. "People were murdered, right here in my apartment! That's a very big deal!"

"Like you said, murders take place every day. In fact it's hard to find an apartment where nothing ever took place, ranging from domestic violence to petty crime to murder." When his mother gave him a look that could kill, he added, "The price was right, and besides, do you know how hard it is to find two adjacent apartments for sale at the same time? You wanted to live right next door to me, remember? So when Dad found these apartments—"

"Your father! *He* found this apartment! He knew!"

"Of course Dad knew. He was in charge of the murder investigation."

"What?!"

Darian shrugged. "This all happened a long time ago, Mother."

"I can't live here anymore," she declared solemnly. "This apartment is dead to me."

"Like its former inhabitants," Jarrett murmured, intently studying the ceiling.

"Why make a big fuss about this now?" Darian asked. "You've lived here for months without a problem and so have I. Nothing has changed, Mother."

"Something has," she said in a low voice. "The spirits have awakened."

"Something must have disturbed them," opined Deshawn.

"Something or someone," added Jarrett with a nasty look at Darian.

"Were there murders in your apartment too?" asked Harry now.

"Not that I'm aware of," Darian replied. And when the others looked at him in consternation, he cried, "It doesn't matter, all right? The dead are dead and buried and life goes on. I don't care if dozens were murdered in my apartment. It won't make me lose a minute of sleep, to be honest."

Harry groaned at this. Sleep. She had the distinct impression that after this she would never sleep again. Nor, apparently, did Em, for she said, "I'm not staying here one second longer, Darian! After this? Not one second!"

"Mother!" said Darian with a look of warning he'd perfected.

"No way," she said, pressing her lips together. "First this apartment needs to be cleansed from these ghoulish intruders."

"They're not really intruders if they were here first," Jarrett pointed out.

She stared at him. "You're absolutely right, Jarrett. Which means I certainly have no business here. I'm moving out, and so are you, Darian!"

"You've got to be joking!" cried her son.

"We're going apartment hunting again first thing in the morning, and you better find me something murder-free this time, or it's your corpse they'll be dragging from the Thames next."

"We can't move simply because you got slimed by some prankster!"

"Watch me!" she said, and stalked out. Then, seeming to remember she had no place to go, she returned, and directed a keen look at Harry. "All right if I move in with you, Harry? Just until that duplicitous son of mine has found me a new place to live?"

"Sure, Em," she said. "Though I have to warn you it's a little small."

"I don't mind small. Small is cozy. The important question is: is it murder-free?"

"I guess so. Apart from Sir Geoffrey Buckley I've never seen any ghosts."

"Why don't you all stay with me?" Jarrett suggested. "I have a very large suite at the Ritz-Carlton that I'm sure you will enjoy very much, Em."

"Oh, that's ever so nice of you, Jarrett," said Em, "but I'm sure Harry's place will be most accommodating, and it will be nice to have my own personal ghost hunter close by in case any more ghosts decide to attack me."

"As you wish," said Jarrett with a smile. "What about you, Darian? Do you need a place to stay? I have a very big bed," he added. "We could spoon."

But Darian held up a hand. "I'm fine, thanks," he said in a voice that betrayed his reluctance to share either a room or a bed with Jarrett, even if it was a suite at the Ritz-Carlton, that fine establishment. "I, for one, don't believe in ghosts, and I will sleep perfectly soundly in my own bed tonight."

"Actually I think we should all stay here tonight," now stated Deshawn. When the others all stared at him, he explained, "In case the wraiths return it's imperative we communicate with them and find out what they want."

Jarrett nodded his assent. "Very well put, Deshawn. We shall camp out here tonight."

"Oh, no," said Em adamantly. "I'm not staying here one more night."

"You can stay at my place tonight, Mother," said Darian, showcasing a nice display of filial affection that Harry, for one, thought was touching.

Em wavered and gave Harry a hesitant look. It was obvious she wasn't yet ready to forego the comfortable option of lodging in Harry's cozy nook.

"I'll be right here," Harry said soothingly. "I'll stay with you tonight, and if something happens, I'm right here to deal with it, all right?"

Em nodded, satisfied with the guarantee. "All right. I'll stay here then."

"Deal," said Harry with a comforting grin.

"What about my apartment?" asked Darian, whose invitation was still standing.

Em waved a hand. "I wouldn't want to be seen dead in your apartment, Darian," she said, choosing her words rather unwisely, Harry felt. "Quite possibly you have the worst interior decorator in the world. The place is a genuine crime against humanity and should probably be the subject of a thorough investigation by the International Court of Justice in The Hague."

Jarrett emitted a fruity chuckle at this, which earned him an unpleasant scowl from Darian. Then Harry's eyes met the inspector's, but they both quickly looked away again. "Let's go," she now said, breaking the awkward silence that had fallen over the company after Em's critical remarks on her son's taste in interior decoration. "We have two more customers to visit."

"And two more ghouls to assuage," added Jarrett.

"If you don't mind I'm going to bed," grumbled Darian.

"No, we don't mind," said Jarrett with a smile.

But Harry said, "Could you ask your dad what happened here?"

He gave her a dubious look, but then finally nodded. "I'll look into it."

"Thanks," she said warmly, and meant it, too.

He seemed on the verge of saying something but then thought better of it. Nevertheless, she thought she could detect the hint of a smile playing about his lips, and knew that even though he professed to be a ghost skeptic, he wasn't going to stand in their way when trying to discover the truth.

"'I'm going with you," said Em, sliding her arm through

Harry's. "I'm not staying here by myself," she added when she gave her a questioning look.

And then, Em attached to her arm like a mollusk, she strode from the apartment. Three hauntings in one night. She had her work cut out for her.

And while Deshawn and Jarrett went ahead, and Em showed them the way, Harry suddenly found herself alone in the corridor with Darian. He was playing idly with his keys, hesitating before moving into his own apartment next door while she closed Em's apartment with the keys she'd handed her.

"So..." said Darian, clearing his throat. "It's been quite a night, huh?"

"And it's not over yet," she pointed out.

He stood gazing at her for a moment, then suddenly blinked and burst out, "I've been meaning to call you, Harry. To, um... to apologize, actually."

She made a throwaway gesture and said, "That's not necessary."

"No, I mean... I said some things I didn't mean last time and.... well..."

"I said some things that I didn't mean," she said softly, staring at her feet.

When she looked up, she found that he was smiling at her, and she was blown away. He'd always had such a charming smile. It was just that lately she hadn't seen much of it. So she smiled back, and he said, "Friends?"

She quickly nodded, and had to fight to speak around the lump that had suddenly formed in her throat. "Friends," she finally croaked, and turned on her heel even as he turned on his. She turned again when he spoke again.

"Um, Harry? Do you want to... grab a bite to eat sometime?"

"Sure," she said. "You've got my number."

"I do," he grinned, then stepped into his apartment and closed the door.

She sighed. Getting over this man wasn't going to be easy.

But then perhaps she didn't even have to?

Chapter 11

The moment Jarrett stepped into the apartment of Bruna Mars, he had the impression he'd entered a different, uglier world. The walls weren't decked with nicely framed pictures of smiling, happy family members but with crudely tin-tacked tacky posters depicting faraway lands, invariably offering bright views of white sandy beaches, clear blue seas and palm trees. The logos of the travel agencies where the posters had been pinched still very much in evidence. And if that wasn't enough to bring the frown to Jarrett's brow, the predominance of chintz certainly did. Chintz curtains, chintz-upholstered sofas, chintz wallpaper... if he'd been a poet, a profession he hadn't tried his hand at yet, he'd have said all this chintz made him wince.

Bruna Mars herself was a kind and hearty woman, easily twice as large as Jarrett's own scrawny frame, and when she laughed, her body shook and so did the walls. Her little girl, who'd seen the ghost in the kitchen, seemed like a real live wire, for if the presence of a ghost in her apartment had rattled her, she didn't give any indication. She actually seemed happy with all the fuss, and probably couldn't wait to share the tale of her ordeal with her friends at school tomorrow.

"Show me the ghost," he now said in his most professional wraith wrangling voice.

Bruna gestured at the kitchen. "I haven't been in there since, but last time we saw him he was making a mess in there, demanding meat for some reason." She shook her head in dismay. "Bloody meat eaters. There should be a law against them. Even when they're dead they can't control themselves."

Since he was a meat eater himself, Jarrett decided not to comment. It was obvious Bruna and he would never see eye to eye on that particular topic. He directed a keen eye at the kitchen, only now becoming aware of the distinct distaste he felt toward the wraithly species. Not for the first time since entering this venture with Harry, he was having second thoughts.

Wrangling spirits was all fine and dandy when discussing the topic in the safety and wraith-free environment of his Rolls Royce or his suite, but now that he was actually getting down to the nitty-gritty and wading knee-deep in nasty wraiths making an absolute mess of things, he felt that perhaps he should leave the more challenging aspects of the business to Harry and Deshawn while he thought deep thoughts about the future of the enterprise.

Harry's boots could be the ones that were on the ground, in other words, while his would be the brains behind the whole operation. Then again, he hadn't come all this way to turn back now, and when both Bruna and Ella Mars directed hopeful looks at him, admiration and anticipation nicely blended on their faces, he thought this was probably what it felt like to be Superman or Batman or Spiderman or anyone with a contingent of admirers cheering them on. So he took a deep breath and said, "Deshawn, you better go and have a look," and gave his man a gentle shove in the right direction.

Deshawn gave him a slightly hurt look, the look of a soldier being reduced to cannon fodder by one of his more cavalier superior officers, but still did as he was told, and stepped boldly where Bruna and Ella had stepped before and entered the kitchen.

Em, who wasn't keen on ghosts after being used for target practice by one of their breed, had decided to hang back and chat with Bruna, reinforcing the bonds of neighborliness and fellow wraith victims.

"Well?" he now asked from the safety of the living room. "Any sign of the foul ghoul?"

Deshawn's hollow voice indicated he wasn't happy with his new role in the Zephyr-Thornton household, but Jarrett was blithely oblivious. In life, his father had always taught him, there are masters and slaves, and Deshawn obviously belonged to the last category while he belonged to the first.

"This place needs a good cleaning," said Deshawn with obvious distaste.

"Do not state the obvious, Deshawn," he said with a touch of irritability. "But does it also need a wraith wrangler? That is the pertinent question."

"Well, no, sir, it doesn't. At least not from where I'm standing."

From where Jarrett was standing all he could see was a poster inviting him to 'Fly to Hawaii for your Hawaiian holiday!', which wasn't very helpful, so he slowly extended his head like a giraffe and peeked behind the kitchen door. All he could see was the wide expanse of Deshawn's back, which finally provided him with the courage he needed to venture deeper into the danger zone. And what he saw there frankly shocked and appalled him.

As Deshawn had indicated, someone had made a terrible mess, depositing the entire contents of the fridge on the checked tile floor for some reason.

"Are you quite sure this was the doing of a ghost, Deshawn?"

Deshawn bent down next to the pile of foodstuffs, now obviously unfit for human consumption, and remarked, "Well, sir, it would appear so." He poked a careless finger at a sausage which lay forlorn amongst a smattering of broken eggs, their yolks smeared about like a finger painting. "It would appear all of this has recently passed the digestive tract of a wraith, sir, as it is now liberally mixed with green slime as you can see if you take a closer look."

Jarrett, who was now pinching his nose with thumb and index finger, said in a nasal tone, "No, thank you, Deshawn. I respectfully decline. It's obvious that green is the predominant color in this tableau, is it not?"

"Indubitably, sir," confirmed Deshawn, now swiftly rising to his feet.

"Which begs the question: if the contents of the ghoul's stomach is on such visually displeasing display, where is the possessor of this stomach?"

"Vanished, sir, after having eaten his fill," opined Deshawn.

"Not very polite, is it? I mean to say, it's not very British to raid a person's fridge, regurgitate the food like your run-of-the-mill fashion model, and then leave without a word of gratitude to the hostess who put up such a feast."

"Very rude indeed, sir."

"I dislike this fiend in ghostly shape already. What say you?"

"I say that Mrs. Mars and her daughter have a serious problem, sir."

Both men stared at the floor where the remains of the wild party lay.

"Which only serves to teach us a lesson, Deshawn: never invite a ghost to your party. Not only will he drive away the other guests and hog all the food, but he will leave a perfect bloody mess. So how do we get rid of this boor?"

"We need to protect the inhabitants of this apartment from

the boor, sir."

"Put them up at the Ritz until we can blow the all-clear, you mean?"

"That would be my suggestion, sir."

"Right," he said, wondering what his father would have to say about footing the bill for his son's wraith wrangling clients. But then he figured that, like all great problems that befall us, this would only serve to make Jarrett Zephyr-Thornton II more spiritual. "Let's put them on the guest list, Deshawn, while Harry figures out a way to make this apartment safe for democracy once again."

"Excellent thinking, sir," said Deshawn, always one to give praise where praise was due.

They returned to the living room, where Ella was watching television now—some inappropriate show about the burial rituals of the Amazonian indigenous tribes—and Em still stood shooting the breeze with Bruna.

"We're going to take you to my place so you can recover from your ordeal," he announced blithely when the two women raised their faces expectantly to the returning hero, not unlike Scarlett O'Hara and Melanie Hamilton awaiting Ashley Wilkes's return from the battlefield. But the news wasn't well received, for Bruna's face revealed her displeasure.

"But I can't just upset my life, Mr..."

"Zephyr-Thornton the Third. But you can call me Jarrett. A few of my friends do," he said with a genial smile.

"If I were you I'd take him up on his offer," said Em. "He lives at the Ritz-Carlton." She then cast a disparaging look around. "Though I can understand why you'd want to stay here. I'd have a hard time too saying goodbye to so much... chintz."

"The Ritz?" Bruna asked, visibly surprised. "Well, that's fine, I guess, but what about Ella? She has school tomorrow, and I have to get to work. I work at a travel agency," she added, confirming one of Jarrett's suspicions.

"Not an issue," said Jarrett. "My man will take you in the Rolls. So pack up whatever you need for this small vacation, and let's get going, shall we?"

"What about the monster?" asked Bruna.

He hesitated, then confidently stated, "Leave it to Harry. It's what I do."

Chapter 12

Harry, who arrived just as Bruna and Ella were leaving with Deshawn, was glad to find that mother and daughter were both unharmed. She didn't think these ghosts would actually hurt the living, but then her experience with the ectoplasmic breed was limited, of course. When she heard of the new arrangement, where Deshawn would escort Bruna and Ella to the Ritz and provide them with a bed for the night, she said, "Oh," and directed a questioning look at her partner-in-crime Jarrett. Was he also leaving?

She remembered that he'd stayed in Em's apartment once before, and hadn't enjoyed the experience, and now wondered if he'd bail on her.

But then they arrived at their next port of call, the home of the Horrocks family, and Harry was pleasantly surprised by the cozy atmosphere they'd managed to create. Even though the floor plan of every apartment was more or less identical, each tenant or owner ran with it and created their own style. It was a rewarding aspect of her new position as wraith wrangler that she was afforded a peek into the personal lives of so many different Londoners.

Mörten, a bespectacled man with thinning sandy hair and a serious expression on his pale face, showed them into the bedroom, where the apparition had apparently made its appearance, and while the conductor and his wife Tamatha, a slight woman with Asian aspect, stood looking on, and Jarrett, Deshawn and the others converged in the living room, she knelt down next to the bassoon case, which was now covered in the same muck Em had experienced before. In fact it was very easy to follow the trajectory of the spray as it extended out from the corner and left a trail of at least six feet.

Dexter would have had a field day mapping out the splatter pattern, even though this was gunk and not blood, obviously, so it might not have appealed all that much to that friendly neighborhood serial killer. Once again, she could pick up nothing, as the ghost had come and gone and refused to show her wraithly face. She finally declared defeat and stood. "I think I need to come back later... alone," she told the couple, who stood hugging each other.

"We both have to be at a very important reception," Mörten said, his face displaying his concern. "Is there any way for you to stay here while we go? You'll be all alone and, um, be able to do whatever it is that you do."

She gave him a reassuring smile. "Sounds like a good idea." In her limited experience ghosts were usually very timid creatures, and didn't feel comfortable showing their faces to a crowd of onlookers. "I think I'll have a better chance at catching this particular wraith when it's just me here."

The woman looked at her with eyes wide. "Aren't you afraid of it?"

Harry laughed. "There's really nothing to be afraid of. Ghosts rarely wish to hurt their living counterparts. They are simply lost beings, with some unfinished business on this shore. Once you figure out what it is they're after, they're happy to move on. Which is where my partner and I come in."

"When we come back tonight…" Mörten began hesitatingly.

"I can't promise you that the apartment will be clear," she said.

"I don't want to sleep here with this monster, Mörten," said Tamatha.

"Me neither," echoed the man with a look of distaste on his face.

Harry wondered whether to tell her that ectoplasm was both a great exfoliant and moisturizer. She had the feeling it wouldn't do much good.

"If you want you can go and stay with my colleague tonight. He's already putting up some of your neighbors. He's got a suite at the Ritz-Carlton."

"Oh," said the conductor, well pleased. "That's so nice of you, Miss…"

"McCabre. Harry McCabre."

They joined the others in the living room and she was pleased that Jarrett immediately agreed to take in two more charges for the night. And as she watched Deshawn leave with the Marses and the Horrockses, she was surprised to find that Jarrett stayed behind. So he wasn't leaving her to her devices after all? His next words confirmed this. "I've convinced Em to spend the night at the Ritz as well. Help the others settle in. Deshawn will drive them over and tuck them in for the night, while you and I stay behind and try to persuade these ghosts to play ball." She was so pleased it must have shown on her face, for he grinned. "What?! Did you really think I was going to leave you here to deal with these ghouls all by yourself?!"

She nodded wordlessly, not trusting her voice at this point.

"I have to confess the prospect of being sprayed with green goo gives me the willies."

"But it's so good for you complexion!" she cried. "I told you already!"

He gave her a slightly supercilious look. "There's absolutely nothing wrong with my complexion, and I certainly don't need green goo to improve it. In any case, I told Em that next time some ghostly fiend directs its projectile vomit at her, she should duck. It will save her a lot of trouble."

"You're right. It's one of those things we should write in our manifesto."

"When being attacked by a ghost, duck," he said appreciatively. "I like it. Succinct and practical. Keep them coming, Harry. You're on fire tonight."

"I'll make a mental note of it," she said.

Then they both turned to the bedroom, where the ghostly ghoul had first manifested. "So how do you propose we go about this?" he asked.

She let out a long stream of air. "I have absolutely no idea."

Chapter 13

Darian was back to pacing his apartment. Though he'd brazenly declared to have no further business with this ghost business, he was already regretting taking the high road. Or was it the low road? Whatever road he'd taken, he'd been in the thick of things before and now he was nowhere. He'd willingly excluded himself from the conversation. A conversation that that nincompoop Jarrett would dominate from now on. And what was more, he was pretty sure that Jarrett was going to poison Harry's mind against him, if he hadn't done so already.

He was the Scotland Yard man on the scene! He should have been the one to take charge of the situation and boss the others around, instead of allowing them to railroad him into bowing out and leaving them to run the show. He couldn't very well go out there now and try to reassert his leadership. Not after having voluntarily relinquished it in the first place.

And then there was his complicated relationship with Harry, of course. He had feelings for her, feelings that ran a lot deeper than mere friendship allowed, and he wondered how she felt about him. They'd never gotten that far in the brief relationship they'd explored, and to her he probably was simply one more notch on her belt. An attractive young woman like her probably had plenty of notches on plenty of belts and by now she'd probably forgotten all about him already. Though she'd accepted his dinner invitation, that didn't necessarily mean anything. It just meant she was a woman who needed to eat, and didn't mind doing it with him picking up the tab.

Oh, well, if she wanted nothing more than mere friendship, nothing more than mere friendship was what she'd get, he thought bravely, though he had to admit mere friendship was not what he wanted. But then why had he broken off relations with her in the first place? Because of her insistence of associating herself with this sordid ghost hunting business. As a Scotland Yard inspector he simply couldn't be connected with such nonsense. If word spread that he was dating Harry McCabre, of Wraith Wranglers fame, he'd be the laughing stock of the force. He'd lose the respect of his subordinates.

He'd walk into a briefing and instead of watching the faces of the men and women he led light up with the light of respect and admiration and a willingness to put their lives on the line, they'd simply snicker and sneer.

That kind of thing puts a damper on one's authority. And career prospects.

He sank down on his black leather couch and propped his feet up on the chrome-and-glass coffee table, the one his mother hated so much, and stared at the black wall with its large chrome studs. And as he stared at the studs, each about a foot in diameter, he wondered if his mother didn't have a point? This place was indeed an interior decorator's worst nightmare. And as he was staring at the wall, subjecting it to a look of scrutiny, he suddenly thought he saw movement. One of the studs seemed to shimmer.

He rubbed his eyes. He was simply tired, that was all. After a long day at the office to come home to all this ghost mess was too much for him. All he needed was a good night's sleep and in the morning he'd be right as rain.

He'd feel differently about all of this and would probably have found a solution for his problems. One solution was obvious: not get involved with Harry again. Easier said than done, for he liked her. A lot. And he'd missed her and would give anything to have her back in his life, crazy ghost hunting nonsense and all.

He opened his eyes again and blinked. The shimmer hadn't diminished. Quite the opposite. Now it appeared as if the entire wall was moving! Christ, what was going on? But before he could jump up from the couch, a face suddenly jumped out from the wall, right next to the flatscreen TV!

It was a leering, nasty face. The face of a middle-aged man, greasy strands of hair dangling from his skull, and a lower jaw that jutted out at odd angles.

"Why don't you get lost?" the face asked in a grating voice, and then, to Darian's consternation, an entire person stepped out from his wall! It was a body that fit with the face: that of a scrawny man. He eyed him malevolently, and croaked, "What are you doing in my house, you numbnuts?"

"This—this is *my* house," he managed to mutter. He was still glued to the couch, his hands pressing into the soft leather, his feet on the coffee table and trying to push himself and the couch away from the approaching figure. Unfortunately the couch was a sturdy clawfoot contraption, its feet digging into the dark concrete floor his designer had assured him was the latest trend.

The figure was still drawing closer, eyeing him balefully. "I want to know what you're doing here?" he now asked, his gray hair dangling lifelessly from white, veiny skin stretched taut over bone. He looked around, as if seeing the room for the first time.

"And I want to know what you did to my house."

"I—I'll have you know this is the latest fashion," he said feebly.

"I filled this house with wooden handicraft. Things I made myself. What did you do with them?" He pointed at the concrete floor. "Where's the parquet I laid with my own hands?" He pointed at the ceiling. "And where are the planks I placed?" He strode around, his jaw working. "I don't recognize this place. You turned it into something ugly. Something very ugly indeed." Finally he pointed a bony finger at him. "And I hold you responsible, you hear? I hold you responsible for what happened to Brunskill Manor!"

"Well, it's my apartment and I can do whatever I want," he said defiantly.

The visitor was walking around now, inspecting Darian's decoration choices with a nasty gleam in his eye, and then, when he'd fingered the massive concrete chicken that 'really tied the room together,' according to the decorator, the corners of his mouth dropped in a vicious scowl. "I told her not to get involved with him," he muttered, more to himself than to Darian. "She knew how I felt and then of course she sent them. Him and that foul friend of his. The animals," he mumbled, balling his skeletal hands into fists. "And then it happened," he said dreamily, his sunken eyes now staring into the distance as if seeing a vista that was hidden to Darian. "And then it happened," he repeated, his face softening. "They took them all away from me. They took everything. They took… my family." Suddenly he directed a look so forlorn at Darian that he gasped. "Help… me?" he asked with quaking voice, holding out a hand. "Help me find… my family?"

Darian found himself nodding. "I will help you," he said, though he had no idea what the other was talking about.

The man smiled a wistful smile. "Thank you, young man. You

may have terrible taste, but you have a good heart. Now where was I?" he asked, pottering back to the wall. "Oh, yes, that's right," he muttered, and then simply walked into the wall and disappeared from sight.

Darian let out a shaky sigh, as he stared, wide-eyed, at the point where the man had disappeared, half expecting him to return. But nothing stirred. Only now did he notice that he was drenched with sweat, and that his heart was beating about a mile a minute.

A ghost, he thought. He'd just seen a ghost! Oh, God! Harry was right! His mother was right! They were all... right! Ghosts... they did exist!

He got up from the couch, and for a moment feared his legs wouldn't be able to support him, but then he was staggering over to the table and picked up his GSM, and then he was flicking through to the third person on his speed dial list. The first was reserved for Harry, the second for his mother, and the third for...

"Dad? It's me, Darian. I need to talk to you. Right now."

Chapter 14

They were back in Em's apartment. It was time to draw up a battle plan, Jarrett had said, though Harry preferred to use the word 'approach.' They needed to find a way to deal with no less than three ghost sightings in one evening, and somehow clean these apartments. Encourage the wraiths to move along now, and leave the present occupants in peace.

And as Harry plunked down on Em's couch, she could hear Jarrett rooting around in the kitchen.

"What are you doing in there?" she asked with a chuckle. She'd be too embarrassed to snoop around another person's flat, but obviously not Jarrett.

"I'm hungry!" came his lament, as he opened the fridge. There was a momentary silence, then she heard bottles clinking merrily and plastic wrapping being ripped open. "Wow, Em's got a fully stocked fridge. I wonder if she's about to start organizing her famous parties again."

"Were they a lot of fun?" she asked, playing with a lock of her hair. She was trying to decide whether to let her hair grow or keep it in a bob like her cousin Alice. They'd always worn their hair the same style, but since her life was sent into a tailspin, she felt like experimenting with her looks. And locks.

"Oh, yes, they were great fun," Jarrett now shouted from the kitchen.

He returned with a tray loaded with stuff and handed her a huge cup with a picture of William and Kate. When she took it she saw it was filled to the brim with chocolate milk, her favorite. It even had marshmallows in it. He himself had his fingers wrapped tightly around a can of Coke Zero.

He placed the tray on the coffee table. It contained Gouda cheese cubes, cheese straws, cocktail sausages, mustard... A lot of finger food for two rumbling stomachs. Wrestling wraiths was apparently good for the appetite.

"So why did she stop throwing them?" she asked, taking a long sip of the sweet beverage and licking her lips delightedly.

"Her divorce, mainly," said Jarrett, settling back on the couch next to her. "After she got divorced and moved here I guess she didn't feel like partying."

"Pity," murmured Harry, who would have liked to attend one of Em's fabled parties.

"They were mostly attended by Scotland Yardies," he said, "and I guess it wasn't much fun for her to see her husband's ex-colleagues all the time."

"Any chance of a reconciliation?" she asked. She was ever the hopeless romantic, wishing people would simply reconcile and get back together.

He shrugged. "Who cares, really? I don't think Em will ever let us look into her heart, but as far as I know that story's definitely ancient history."

"So what happened?"

He frowned. "Well, as far as I can tell—and mind you, your honor, that this is merely hearsay and conjecture—her husband cheated on her with his secretary. When she found out it was game over for Chief Inspector Watley."

She gasped and shook her head. "Not his secretary?"

"Well, not exactly. I made that up. I think it was his yoga teacher."

"How terrible. I'll bet she was all young and bendy."

"She was bendy, all right, but barely young. She was about Broderick's age, I should think."

"Broderick? Is that Darian's dad's name?"

"Indeed it is. Chief Inspector Broderick Watley of the Yard. The one and only. Mind you, I never managed to get Em to confirm or deny any of this."

"I feel so sorry for her. She's such a great person, and such a classy lady."

"Yeah, she sure is," Jarrett said, taking a long swig from his can and then placing the cool container against this temple. "Listen, darling, as much as I love gossiping about other people—and I have to confess it's one of my favorite pastimes—don't you think we need to come up with some kind of battle plan? How to rid these apartments of these unruly dead, I mean?"

She nodded. It was much easier to gossip about Em's failed marriage than to actually figure out what to do. "I guess you're right," she said. "It's just that…" She lifted her hands ineffectually. "I have no clue what to do!"

"Well put. And you should have added, 'Neither do you!'"

"I mean, last time we did this we had a lot of help, remember?"

He leaned back. "Buckley was still around, and that American fellow."

"Peverell Wardop." The multi-billionaire owner of the Wardop group, now deceased, had been a great help. But both Buckley and Peverell had moved on, apparently, and now it was just her and Jarrett.

"I tried to get in touch with these spirits and... nothing. Zilch. Not even a tiny blip on my ghost radar. Do you think I lost my touch? That ghosts simply don't respond to me anymore? That I'm a wraith wrangler no more?"

"I think that's pretty much out of the question, darling. You are, bar none, the greatest wraith wrangler I've ever met. Of course you're also the only wraith wrangler I've ever met."

"Thanks, I guess," she said dubiously.

"You know what would help? If we had some clue about the history of this place. I mean, these ghosts didn't just pop up for no reason. They must be connected with this building. If we could only talk to someone who was around when these murders took place, we might glimpse some context."

"You mean Darian's dad. He was around, apparently."

"What did Darian say? Was he going to ask him about the investigation?"

Harry nodded. She had her doubts about Darian's promises, though. He didn't believe in ghosts and wouldn't touch the wispy breed with a ten-foot pole—figuratively speaking, of course, for ghosts rarely enjoy being touched with ten foot poles or any other objects. And it wasn't merely ghosts the inspector abhorred touching. She also fell under the embargo, apparently. He'd asked her out to dinner, but she knew better than to read too much into it. He probably just wanted to be on cordial terms with a friend of his mother.

"He asked me out to dinner," she now said, glancing at Jarrett.

"Ooh, you're getting it on again," he said with a grin.

"I doubt it," she said, idly rolling her tresses between her fingers. "I think he was just trying to be nice to me. Because Em likes me so much."

But Jarrett shook his head decidedly. "Uh-uh. No way, darling. If I'm anything I'm a keen judge of character, and that man is still severely smitten."

She blushed at this. "No, he's not. He's the one who walked out and never called me again. That's not the behavior of a smitten man."

"It is exactly the behavior of a smitten man," countered Jarrett. "He sees that this ghost thing is coming between him and you and decided to give you an ultimatum: drop the Wraith Wranglers or drop me."

She frowned. "What are you saying?"

"That if you'd called him and told him this love affair between you and the wispy ones was over, he'd have been at your door before you'd put down the phone, panting and wagging his tail like a lovesick puppy."

She laughed at the image of Darian Watley wagging his tail and looking like a lovesick puppy. It did something to her insides, though she wasn't going to admit that to Jarrett. "I really don't think…"

"And I really do," he stressed. "Trust me on this. You may know everything there is to know about ghosts—"

"Well…"

"—but I know a thing or two about men—my area of expertise," he added with a wink. "And if you want my opinion—and even if you don't, I'm going to give it to you—Darian Watley is a cutie pie and deeply enamored."

She eyed him uncertainly. "I don't think I want your opinion about Darian, Jarrett."

"Like I said, you're getting it anyway," he said, holding up his can of Coke, "and free of charge no less. I think the only thing stopping that man from barging in here and grabbing you in his arms and pressing a thousand kisses on your upturned face is pride. As a Scotland Yardie he's got a lot to lose, and getting involved with a known wraith wrangler presents a definite career risk. So now he's got to choose between love or money." He held up his hands like weighing scales, balancing the options. "Love or money, babe."

"And what is he going to choose?" she asked a little breathlessly.

"Love, of course. Eventually," he admitted. "The guy's not very smart, so it might take him a while to see the light. Like most coppers, and in spite of whatever else he's got going for him—and I'll grant you that the man is hot—he's your typical copper: solid ivory from the neck up, if you catch my drift."

"So... You're saying there's still hope for me?"

He smiled at her and patted her knee affectionately. "There's plenty of hope for you, young lass. Just you wait and see. Sooner or later Darian Watley will keep you warm at night once more, and when the wedding bells finally ring out, I'll be the first to chuck a cup of rice in your face. Where are you going for your honeymoon?" He held up a hand before Harry could respond. "And please don't book your trip with Bruna Mars. I have a feeling she'll sell you on Hawaii, and there's so many other places you could pick."

"Don't you have some private island we could go to?" she asked dreamily.

"You mean like Richard Branson? Afraid not, darling. Dad was never that cool." He grimaced. "Never too keen on waterskiing with naked women on his back, and neither am I, for that matter. Though if pushed I could be persuaded to go for a naked Darian Watley on my back," he conceded.

"Yew!" she cried, slapping his leg. "If a naked Darian Watley is going to be on anybody's back it's going to be mine, Jarrett! And mine alone!"

He laughed. "And we're back, ladies and gentlemen!" he announced.

"Back to square one," she said with a sigh. "We still don't know what to do about these ghosts."

"I know what to do about these ghosts," suddenly a stentorian voice sounded from the vestibule, and both Harry and Jarrett looked up, greatly surprised and half expecting a ghost to suddenly drift into their field of vision. Instead, it was Darian Watley. Only he wasn't naked, and judging from the somber look on his face he wasn't ready to go waterskiing either.

Chapter 15

"And for your information," he said, directing a pointed look at Jarrett, "I'm not dumb."

"Oops," said Jarrett with a grin.

"And for your information," he added, now looking at Harry, "I do know how to waterski, though I have to admit I've never tried it in the nude."

Her cheeks instantly flamed with color, and she was suddenly feeling both hot and cold. "We were just joking," she murmured, casting down her eyes.

"Or daydreaming," clarified Jarrett. Then he patted a spot on the sofa next to him. "Take a load off, darling. Join us for a meeting of the board."

"I know what happened in this house," Darian now said, ignoring Jarrett's invitation but instead opting to remain standing. He rather looked like a majestic tree as he stood there, wide-legged. An emperor of the forest.

"You have the floor, old man," said Jarrett graciously. "Take it away."

"I called my dad just now, and he told me this building was one big house, and the home to one single family."

"One family?" Harry asked, surprised.

"That's right. The Pringles. One night, thirty-five years ago, they were all brutally killed, all ten of them. The house was later divvied up into nine separate apartments and rented out."

Jarrett whistled through his teeth. "A slaughterhouse, huh? Who knew?"

"My dad, apparently," grumbled Darian. "And he should have told us."

Even he seemed uncomfortable with the idea of living in a house of horrors, Harry saw. And now that she came to think of it, he actually looked as if he'd just seen a ghost. A little rattled, and a little pale around the nostrils.

"You said you knew how to deal with these ghosts?" she asked.

"That's an aspect of the matter that puzzles me," said Jarrett. "Correct me if I'm wrong, but it was my impression you didn't believe in ghosts, Darian."

Darian gave them both a silent stare, then abruptly turned on his heel and stalked off to a small cabinet near the wall. He opened it to reveal a mini bar. Or rather a maxi bar, as it seemed to hold quite a nice array of bottles.

"Oh, Darian," said Jarrett solicitously. "You haven't taken to drink, have you? Things are not that bad. Nothing we can't deal with, right, Harry?"

But Harry was staring at the impressive display of bottles. "I thought you said Em didn't throw parties anymore?" she asked.

"Looks like she lied to me," said Jarrett, pained. "Or else my invitations keep getting lost in the mail."

"Mother doesn't do parties anymore," Darian confirmed, "but she still has friends, and those friends like to have a drink." And to make his meaning clear, he quaffed deeply from an amber-colored liquid that didn't look like Coke or cocoa. It made Harry wonder if Darian and his mother were anonymous alcoholics, but since she knew their names they probably weren't.

"I saw a ghost," said Darian in a low voice, his eyes squeezed tightly shut.

"You saw what?!" cried both Harry and Jarrett, greatly surprised by this shock confession.

"You heard," he muttered, then plunked down on the opposite couch. "A man. He walked into my apartment just now, straight out of the wall, if you please. Asked me why I made so many alterations to the place and why I chucked his woodcraft and his parquet floor and..." He took another gulp of liquor, then continued, "And then he asked me to help him find his family," he said in a slightly ragged voice. He shook his head and now looked at Harry, his gray eyes contrite. "I should never have doubted you, Harry."

"Or me," said Jarrett primly.

"You were right all along. Ghosts... they do exist."

"Well, hallelujah," said Jarrett, slapping his thigh quite inappropriately. "Welcome aboard!" he cried with glee. "I knew you'd see the light eventually!"

Darian shook his head, still dazed and confused, and Harry could readily see why. Especially for a man like Darian, whose life was all cold hard facts and evidence, ghosts were an anomaly that shouldn't exist. But now that he'd seen them with his own two eyes he couldn't deny their existence any longer.

"What did your dad say when you told him about the ghost?" she asked.

"I didn't tell him," he confessed. "I'm not talking about this to anyone and neither should you. As far as the world is concerned, I'm not a believer."

"Oh, but I am," said Jarrett. "A big belieber. And if Justin ever drops by, I'm willing to tell him up close and in person."

"I don't know what to do," confessed Darian. "I've never seen a ghost before. The experience was harrowing. That man... he looked terrible."

"The dead usually do," said Jarrett. "That's why they're called the dead."

"I wonder who he was," mused Harry, "and how he's related to the other ghosts."

"Okay," said Jarrett, sitting up. "So who do we have so far? Girl in the yoga room, who said something about being killed."

"The man in the Bruna Mars kitchen, sitting on the floor. Perhaps a relative?" Harry ventured.

"Or a visitor," Darian said.

"And then there was another little girl in the Horrocks bedroom," said Jarrett, "which makes..." He gazed at the ceiling as his lips moved wordlessly, "about a dozen little girls and half a dozen other ghosts?"

Harry laughed, and even Darian displayed the ghost of a smile.

"We need to use a modicum of logic," the policeman said. "We need to know exactly who lived here and who died here, and then we'll know where we stand."

Jarrett quirked an eyebrow at the esteemed inspector. "We? Did you just use the word 'we?' Do you mean to tell me, my dear Inspector Darian Watley of Scotland Yard, that you have decided to join us on our sacred quest?"

Darian shrugged. "I don't know what I'm doing, to be honest. All I know is that my mother is having trouble meditating, and that she'll refuse to put another foot in this apartment as long as there's even the slightest possibility of a ghost lurking around."

"Even if that ghost is gone, I'm afraid your mother is going to want to move out, darling," said Jarrett. "She's not the type of woman who tolerates an uninvited guest, and most certainly not of the ghostly kind."

"That's too bad," he said, sinking deeper into the couch's pillows and resting his tumbler on his knee, "because finding two halfway decent adjacent units in London for a reasonable price is pretty much impossible these days. We got lucky on this apartment, because Dad pulled some strings, but—"

"Perhaps he got lucky because of the history of the house," Harry ventured.

Darian eyed her morosely. "You're probably right."

"Look. I'm sure I can convince Em to stay," said Harry, "but first we need to rid the apartment of these ghosts. So are you going to help us, Darian?"

He eyed her for the longest time, ratcheting up the suspense like the coaches on *The Voice* before picking a winner, then finally said, "Yes, I am."

Chapter 16

Darian was feeling not a little silly. After all the heated arguments. After trying to convince Harry that she was wrong and he was right. After walking out on her... And now he was forced to admit she was right all along...

He could only imagine what his mother would say. She'd never let him live it down. For the rest of his life—and every time they had an argument—she'd rub his nose in it. 'Remember when you told me ghosts didn't exist? Huh! You were wrong then and you're wrong now!'

Oh, God, he thought as he rubbed his face with his hands. "So what do we do now?" he asked, and when he looked up saw that Jarrett was eyeing him strangely. Well, at least a little more strangely than usual.

"What? Am I wearing something of yours?"

Jarrett merely shook his head, his eyes still riveted on him.

But then he saw that Harry, too, was looking at him as if he had something on his face. "Come on. Out with it," he said brusquely. He was running low on patience after the stirring events that had taken place.

And now he saw that they weren't actually looking at him but a few inches above his head, for some reason. And when he felt a clammy sensation at the back of his neck, the penny dropped. "There's a ghost behind me, isn't there?"

Both Harry and Jarrett slowly nodded, still looking quite stunned.

There was a definite cold front blowing in from the North, the back of his neck experiencing a chill like none he'd ever felt, and spreading fast.

"And it's a big one, isn't it?"

They both nodded again, like two bobbleheads.

"And he's going to slime me, isn't he?"

Even before they could acknowledge this was indeed the case, he felt the first cold, wet gobs of spittle hitting his neck and dribbling down his back!

"Duck!" Jarrett yelled, suddenly released from his stupor, and he and Harry instantly hit the floor. And he was just about to do the same when he got the full blast. It seemed as if a container of slime was tipped over on his head, and then he was screaming bloody murder as he was being slimed like probably no one in the history of ghost encounters has ever been slimed.

It was as if this particular ghost had decided that Darian was a great candidate for the Slime Bucket Challenge and was now giving of his best.

And when Darian finally did hit the floor, he was spluttering and spitting the gooey yuck from his mouth, and felt the icy stuff go through his clothes and hit his bare skin, effectively wrapping him into its frosty blanket.

And then he was crawling to the others, directing a fearful look back at the creature who was doing this to him. And when he finally managed to get a good look at the monster's face, he saw to his surprise that it was...

"Mother!" he cried, getting the words out between two spits of slime.

In response, his mother opened her mouth, and upchucked another truckload of green slime all over him, leaving him howling in agony.

If he was surprised at this twist, Harry and Jarrett even more so, for Harry now asked, "Em, what are you doing?"

And Jarrett chimed in with, "Em, this is no way to treat your guests!"

"Or your son!" he bellowed.

But the woman, who looked as if she'd just reared up from the grave, all chalky white face and bony limbs, seemed verbally challenged, for she simply kept spraying him with goo, as if she'd been saving the stuff up for decades. And when finally she ran out, she quickly turned around and made a dash for the wall, then simply jumped through it and disappeared, leaving a nasty big green stain on her own crepe wallpaper.

Darian, still recovering from the shock of being slimed by his own mother, cried, "This is not happening!"

"Guess what? It just did," said Jarrett soberly.

"But how can she be dead? She was just here!"

"I don't think that was your mother, Darian," Harry's voice interrupted his frazzled thoughts. "She merely looked like her. Or was related to her."

Darian rose, now dripping with goo. The stuff was all over him! In his nose, in his eyes, in his mouth! And soaking straight through his clothes!

"Welcome to the world of wraith wrangling, Darian," said Jarrett solemnly. He was eyeing him with distinct distaste. Then he rubbed at a small drop that had attached itself to his shirt. "Yuck. I got some on me, too."

"We have to do something!" cried Darian indignantly. It wasn't fair, he felt, for the only non-wraith wrangler in the room to be wrangled by a wraith!

"The stains come off easily," said Harry helpfully. "They wash off in the shower. And for your clothes I would suggest washing them at a low temperature." She gave him a beaming smile. "They'll be as good as new." She blinked. "Which reminds me…" She hopped up from the floor and dashed over to take a generous helping of goo from his shirt. "Em likes to use this stuff as a facial mask. Do you suffer from dry skin? No? Oh, all right."

His jaw dropped at this. "How can you be so cool?! I'm terrified!"

"Oh, you get used to them," said Harry airily.

"Yes, after your first dozen, they grow on you," agreed Jarrett.

"You haven't seen a dozen," said Harry. "We only just got started."

"Well, *he* doesn't know!" hissed Jarrett, jerking his thumb at Darian.

"Hey! A little help?!" Darian cried. He was still covered in goo from head to foot, and didn't feel comfortable heading over to his mother's bathroom, dripping all over her carpets. He knew there would be hell to pay if he did.

Jarrett languidly ambled off, to return with a big pink plastic tub Darian's mother used for hand-washing her lingerie. He put it down in front of him, careful not to get any goo on him, and said invitingly, "Step into it."

"What's the big idea?"

"Well, you strip, of course, and drop your clothes into the tub."

Through gritted teeth, he said, "I'm not going to strip, Jarrett."

"Suit yourself," said Jarrett with a careless shrug.

"Guys, we need to figure out how to communicate with these

ghosts," Harry interrupted this gay guy banter. "Now all they seem to want to do is scare us off. What else did your father say, Darian?"

Darian, who'd presided over meetings in all kinds of circumstances, had never run a meeting covered in ectoplasm. But in spite of the circumstances, he decided to make the best of it. So he started scooping off the goo, and depositing it into the plastic receptacle. "Dad said he'd try to wrangle me up the file," he said, choosing his words perhaps a little injudiciously. "He only remembered a few details. Like the fact that all members of the Pringle family died that night."

"Did he ever catch the killer?" asked Harry, now seated once more on the couch and snacking on Gouda cubes. To her this was simply a fun night out, apparently, and Darian was providing the entertainment.

He lifted his shoulders. "No, he never did."

"Great," said Harry with a grin. "So we get to solve a cold case."

"And we better solve it," said Darian. "I don't want to go through this terrible ordeal again."

"You look cute, Darian," commented Jarrett. "Like a snowman, but without the snow. And the hat. And the carrot and the, um, and the scarf." Then he added on a cheerier note, "I think you should simply strip. Don't be shy, darling. Just drop your clothes in the tub and I'll carry you to the bathroom. You can sit on my shoulders, naked. I confess I don't have any waterskiing experience, but then you can't have it all, can you?"

He respectfully declined the offer, and growled, "Is this how you Wraith Wranglers always operate?"

"Yep," confessed Harry, popping another Gouda into her mouth. "Usually we just sit around and wait for inspiration to strike, isn't that right, Jer?"

"Pretty much," Jarrett confirmed. "You see," he added, holding up his finger like a professor about to teach a class the finer points of quantum physics, "wraith wrangling, contrary to what you may have heard, Darian, is not an exact science. It's basically guesswork, and we just go with our gut."

"And fill your gut with my mother's food," he said, "which reminds me..." He wanted to take his phone from his pocket but since he was still covered in slime, instead he asked Harry, "Can you call my mother? See if she's okay? That ghost looked so much like her I just want to be sure she's fine."

"Of course," she said, taking out her own phone and dialing Em's number.

"I don't think it was her," said Jarrett. "She would have looked much fresher. Recently deceased," he corrected when Darian hit him with a scowl.

"Oh, hi, Em? It's so good to hear your voice," Harry said, and Darian breathed a sigh of relief. "Yes, we just had a visit from a ghost who looked just like you. Yes, we're all fine. Your carpets?" She directed a look at the carpet beneath the coffee table, which was now nicely covered in slime. "Well..." She hesitated. "There might be a smudge, but it was Darian who—"

"No!" cried Darian, throwing up his hand in warning and lobbing a big, fat blob of goo at the wall, barely missing Jarrett, who ducked just in time.

"Oh, yes, he's here with us. He was the one who bore the brunt of the attack." She grinned at Darian as she listened, and he could hear his mother's jubilant cries. "Yes, he does believe in ghosts now, Em. Yes, I agree it's a wonderful surprise. He's become a believer now." She listened again, then laughed. "Oh, I will tell him. Of course. Sleep well, Em. See you tomorrow."

Darian directed a piercing glare at her. "What did she say?"

"Well, she said to tell you that you owe her one."

"Owe her what for what?" he snapped irritably.

"Owe her a party. She said you told her once that she'd be able to organize her famous parties again on the day you became a ghost believer. So..."

"Why did you ever forbid Em to throw her parties, Darian?" Jarrett now asked plaintively. "It is one of the great mysteries of our time."

Darian sighed. "Because they made her miserable. After the divorce she insisted on keeping things the same, including her Friday night parties. But every friend she had was a mutual friend with Dad, and they all kept reminding her of the good old days when they were still together. So I told her she needed to get back on her feet first, and that continuing a tradition that was so strongly associated with Dad was never going to get her there."

"Oh, that's kind of sweet," said Harry.

"Yes, Darian," agreed Jarrett. "I never thought you had it in you."

"Had what in me?" he asked, flinging another blob of goo in the tub.

"A heart," Jarrett said, fluttering his eyelashes.

"Ha ha," he muttered. "Well, at least Mother is fine, which is a relief."

"Is it true your dad cheated on Em with his yoga teacher?" Jarrett asked.

"Jarrett!" hissed Harry.

"What? Inquiring minds want to know. In case I ever run into this yoga instructor I can give her a small piece of my mind. Or even a big one."

Darian hesitated, then finally nodded. "There were rumors of an affair, though Dad always denied them vehemently."

"So what do *you* think?" Jarrett now asked.

"Jarrett! We have more important things to do than talk about Em's divorce!"

Darian frowned. "Well, I always thought Mother was too... impetuous when she decided to divorce Dad on the basis of a rumor," he said slowly.

"Did you ever talk to the woman?" Harry now asked. "What?" she asked when Jarrett chuckled. "I also have an inquiring mind. And I love Em, so..."

"Actually I did talk to Caroline Freeby, and she assured me there was no basis in fact. But of course the damage was done. Mother refused to believe it wasn't true and..." He sighed. "If you want to know what I think..."

"Yes, we do want to know what you think, Darian," Jarrett said quickly. He looked like one watching a reality show and waiting for the big finale.

"I think the rumor was started out of petty jealousy. My parents had such a great relationship, and Dad a very successful career. To this day I suspect someone started the rumor and poisoned Mother's mind so that they could drive her and Dad apart." And that, he thought, was all he was ever going to say on the matter, especially to Jarrett, who was a notorious blabbermouth.

"Such a sad tale," said Harry with a wistful sigh. "I wish I could do something. Try to convince Em to give Broderick another chance."

"I'm afraid that ship has sailed," he grunted, then announced, "And now if you don't mind I'm going to take a shower. And when I get back you two better come up with a plan of campaign, because I'm not going to go through this experience again." And then he was off, and he didn't care that he made big, nasty green stains on his mother's carpets. If they couldn't get this pack of nasty ghosts out of here, she was never going to come back here anyway.

"Darian!" Harry called out after him.

He turned. "What?!" He knew he looked like an idiot, with all this slime.

But then she gave him a radiant smile that warmed the cockles of his heart, and some other parts of his anatomy, too. "I'm glad you're on board."

Chapter 17

Broderick crawled out of the cab and stared up at the facade of the house where his son and ex-wife lived. A thickset man with a bristling buzz cut of gray going on white, a white mustache and a face hewn from granite, he'd never been a tolerant man but rather a strict disciplinarian, both in life and on the job. Now, past the age of retirement, when order and discipline mattered more than ever as he adjusted himself to this new reality, Em's shock announcement that she was seeking a divorce had come as a bolt from the blue, fully upending his life.

The former chief inspector liked things a certain way: the house just so, dinner on the table at six, evenings spent in front of the telly, and once a week visiting with a friendly couple. And now this had all fallen apart and he wasn't coping too well, especially since the specious accusations of his wife had no basis in fact. He did not have sexual relations with that woman, Caroline Freeby, and he was prepared to testify to the matter under oath.

Not that it would do him any good. Em didn't believe a word he said and that was that, as far as she was concerned. The divorce wasn't final yet, but it would be in a matter of weeks, and then he'd be a bachelor once again.

And now all this nonsense about some old murder case his son kept bugging him about. And in the middle of the night, no less! Thirty-five years the case file had gathered dust in the archives, and now suddenly Darian wanted him to wrangle him up the file ASAP. When he'd retired, he'd sworn never to set foot inside New Scotland Yard ever again, leaving things to other, more capable—and younger—men, and he'd kept his promise. Until tonight. Why this was suddenly so important he didn't understand, but Darian had insisted he bring him the file personally and immediately.

He didn't like to be ordered about, and most certainly not by a former subordinate. And then of course there was the fact that he tried to steer clear of the building where his soon-to-be-ex-wife now lived. He still resented her upending his life like that, and if he never saw her again it was fine by him.

But Darian had told him that there was no risk whatsoever of running into Em tonight and that it was just him and a couple of his friends, chief amongst whom was the woman Darian had recently befriended, and with whom relations stronger than mere friendship had developed. Until she'd outed herself as a ghost hunter, that was. Like his son, Broderick Watley detested quacks and loonies, and it seemed to him Harry McCabre was both.

He rang the bell of Darian's apartment, and when no one answered the door, he rang again, pressing his finger down on the buzzer with an irritated scowl on his face. "Jiminy cricket," he murmured, and took out his cell.

When the call went straight to voicemail, he cursed again. First Darian practically dragged him out of bed with this lunacy, and now he wasn't even home! What the devil was he playing at? And then suddenly someone did pick up the phone, and he barked, "Darian?! Darian, is that you?! This is your father speaking! Respond immediately!" But instead of his son's voice, a more melodious version responded. A female voice, no less!

"Hello, Mr. Watley. Darian is taking a shower right now. Come on up."

"Who are you? And what are you doing answering my son's phone?!"

"I'm Harry. I'm a friend of Darian's."

"Harry? Harry McCabre?" He wanted to add, 'The fruit loop?' but refrained from doing so. No matter how whacked this female was, apparently she and Darian were still on matey terms.

"That's right. Come on up. Oh, and Mr. Watley? We're in Em's apartment right now so you might want to hang a left when you get up here." And abruptly she disconnected, seeming to feel she'd said all she needed to say.

His frown deepened. No way was he going to visit his wife at this time of night, or any other time for that matter. So he vigorously stabbed at his phone and within seconds was listening to Harry's voice again. She had a nice voice, as voices went, but since he wasn't a coach on *The Voice* he didn't really care one way or another. So he barked, "Is Em up there with you?!"

"Oh, hello again, Mr. Watley. No, Em is staying at the Ritz," she said. "It's just, me, Darian, and Jarrett. Jarrett Zephyr-Thornton?"

"Right," he said with a frown. "Quite so." Now he remembered Darian told him Em had gone out. "I'm coming up," he announced bravely.

"Excellent decision," she said, and pressed the buzzer once again.

The door to Em's apartment was ajar, and he carefully made his way inside, fully expecting to find some sort of wild orgy going on, like in the sixties, when as a young sergeant he was always called upon to break up some hippie luvvie debauchery after receiving a complaint from the neighbors. As it was, no orgy was in progress, and the first sight that greeted him was that of an ordinary and perfectly pleasant-looking young blond woman, seated on the couch with Jarrett Zephyr, whose face he recognized from his frequent insertion in the entertainment section of his newspaper.

But then his eye flew to a pink plastic tub, filled with some sort of lubricant, and the same lubricant was smeared all over the carpet and, as his widening eye traveled beyond the salon, even on the walls! And he was just opening his mouth to speak, when Darian ambled in, stark naked from the waist up, carelessly toweling his hair.

"Oh, hey, Dad," Darian said casually. "Glad you could make it."

"I'm having no part of this," he announced instantly. He would have added he was a married man and not into any kind of kinky stuff, but then of course he'd have been lying. He directed a keen eye at his son. "Does Em know about this... this... this stuff?"

Darian frowned. "What stuff?"

He gestured wildly at the buckets of lubricant. "That stuff!"

"Oh, sure," said Harry now. "We told her all about it."

His eyes widened even more. "And what did she have to say about it?"

"Well, she was surprised, of course," said Harry.

"I should say she was!"

"Especially since it happened to her only hours ago."

"What?!"

"No harm came to her, Mr. Watley," said Jarrett gravely.

"Yes, Dad. Mother is perfectly fine," said Darian, directing meaningful glances at his two cohorts, as if to tell them to shut it.

"This is an outrage!" he cried, gesturing with the file folder.

"Oh, thanks, Dad," said Darian, snatching it from his fingers. "Just what we needed."

"I demand to know the meaning of this!" he demanded, even though he knew perfectly well what the meaning of this was. Jarrett Zephyr-Thornton's mere presence in this apartment was enough to warn him that most untowardly things had been happening here, and, like the young sergeant he'd once been, he was determined to put a stop to it at once!

"The ghosts don't mean anyone any harm, sir," said Harry now, a concerned look on her pretty face. "They're just very confused is all."

It was as if the conversation had just lurched into a different, more surrealistic world, if possible, and he was, frankly, too stunned for speech.

"Harry," said Darian warningly, then directed an apologetic smile at his father. "Don't listen to her. She's got a thing for ghosts, as you may have noticed."

"Ghosts," he rumbled under his breath.

"Funny thing," said Jarrett with a chuckle. "The ghost who attacked Darian just now was the spitting image of Em. Can you imagine? Ha ha!"

But Broderick wasn't laughing. He wasn't even smiling. He was pointing at the lubricant. "Do you mean to tell me that that... residue was left by a... a ghost?!"

"Sure was, sir," said Harry. "But don't worry. It doesn't leave stains."

He directed a censorious look at his son. "What the devil is going on here?"

Jarrett sighed. "Well, Harry is right, Dad. I did see a ghost, and so did a lot of other people in the building, Mother included, and we think their appearance has something to do with the murders that took place here thirty-five years ago." He waved the file folder. "The murders you investigated."

Chapter 18

It was a startling confession from one who, until a few moments ago, had been a ghost skeptic himself, and Harry wondered how Broderick Watley would respond. She didn't have to wait long, for the man's face now turned beet-red, which was not a good sign in her estimation. It appeared as if steam would soon be flowing from his ears, if such a phenomenon was physically possible. And then he puffed up his chest, and seemed on the verge of launching into a long and vituperative tirade, when Jarrett held up a hand.

"I know this must seem very peculiar to you, sir, but I can assure you that your son is not joking. In fact I don't think Darian is capable of joking, as he is a policeman and a sense of humor is not a requirement for that particular job."

This statement only served to infuriate the man even more, and he now resembled one of those World War II bombs, often found by unsuspecting farmers plowing their fields, liable to go off at the slightest provocation.

"What Jarrett means to say," said Harry, "is that ghosts do exist, sir, and both your wife and your son have been the victims of a recent attack."

"It's true, Dad," said Darian, dragging his fingers through his damp hair. "Mother was attacked while she was meditating just before, and now the same thing happened to me, and to two of our neighbors as well."

"But that's preposterous!" finally exploded the retired chief inspector. "That's sheer nonsense! Ghosts… ghosts don't exist, Darian! What you and Emmanuella saw must have been something else. Someone's idea of a practical joke, perhaps," he added, casting a furious glance at Jarrett.

"No, it wasn't. It was a ghost, Dad. I saw it with my own two eyes."

"And the rest of him," added Jarrett cheerfully. "You should have seen him, Broderick, old chum. Your son was soaked to the gills with the stuff!"

"This is an outrage," the chief inspector began, his hands balling into fists and now quivering from stem to stern like a gelatinous custard pudding.

"We should have made a video," said Harry now, addressing Jarrett.

Jarrett's hand flew to his brow. "I knew we'd forgotten something!"

"Look, Dad, I know you don't believe me. Heck, I didn't believe Mother when she told me, or Harry or Jarrett. But I can promise you that it happened and happened right here in this very room. And since it looks like it will keep happening unless we do something about it, we have to act now."

And as Darian opened the file folder, his father stuffed his hands deeply into the pockets of his overcoat and removed himself from the scene with a deep frown etched on his brow. Harry felt for the man. Not only had he lost his wife, due to some nasty gossipmongers, but now he must think both she and his son had lost their marbles. A man would be cross for much less.

So while Jarrett and Darian studied the file, she approached the retired chief inspector a little wearily. "Em's fine, by the way," she told him. "She's staying at Jarrett's to recover from the harrowing experience, along with some of the neighbors who experienced the same strange phenomena."

He merely grumbled something, staunchly refusing to meet her eye.

"It's not the first time this happened to Em," she continued, trudging on regardless, "and I thought she reacted very well on both occasions. Last time she even tried to shoot the apparition with the shotgun you gifted her."

He looked up at this, a gleam of something appearing in his eye. She thought it was surprise and perhaps even pride, but it was hard to be certain.

"She did curse at the fact that the gun wasn't loaded, though," she added.

"Can't give the woman a gun," he grumbled. "She'd shoot the plumber if he dared to overcharge her and then where would she be?"

"In jail, probably," Harry agreed.

"You're telling me Em is all right?" he asked.

"Oh, yes, she's fine. It takes more than a little ghost to rattle Em."

The ex-chief inspector now actually displayed the hint of a smile, and rocked back on his heels, his hands firmly clasped behind his back. "Yes, she's not afraid of anything, Em isn't. Tough as nails, and fearless. Fearless!"

"She's very special, and I'm proud she's my friend," said Harry warmly.

He eyed her a little reluctantly. "So you're a friend of Em's, are you?"

She could see how unlikely that was, not moving in the same social circles at all, so she said, "We shared certain experiences, and it created a bond."

"I just wish she would come to her senses," he grumbled. "This whole divorce business..." He hesitated, and darted a sharp look at her, as if trying to gauge whether she was worthy of his confidences or not.

"Darian told me about that. I was very sorry to hear the story."

"How much did he tell you?"

"Well, that there were certain rumors, and that Em took them very hard."

"Rumors is right," he grunted. "No basis in fact. Just a lot of garbage."

"So this whole story about you and the yoga instructor..."

"Lies!" he huffed. "All lies! I never got involved with any yoga instructor. Was faithful throughout. Only she won't believe me. Says all men are the same. Well, we're not all the same!" he stated emphatically. "Some of us are actually faithful to our wives! And ready to kiss the ground they walk on."

"Yes, I can see that now," she said, believing him. "Do you want me to put in a good word for you? Try to convince her she's making a great mistake?"

His face turned to her, hope suddenly casting it in a beautiful light. "Would you? She won't give me the time of day, but perhaps a friend..."

"I will talk to her," she promised, placing a reassuring hand on the man's arm. He eyed it curiously for a moment, as if the gesture was new to him. And she could see why, of course. None of his underlings would ever place a gentle hand on his arm. It would probably be construed as familiarity. But she felt for the man, and as she was a hopeless romantic, she felt here was a project she could devote herself wholeheartedly to.

"Do you really believe in ghosts?" he now asked, darting a quick look at his son, who stood bent over the file folder.

"It's not so much a matter of belief, as simply a matter of experience. Once you've seen your first ghost you'll see what I mean," she told him.

"I won't ever see my first ghost," he said, some of the old crustiness returning. "For ghosts simply don't exist, young lady."

She merely smiled at him. After having met quite a few skeptics, she knew that arguing was a waste of time. These non-believers needed to see, and their skepticism would vanish like the snow on the Kilimanjaro. And then suddenly the door swung open, and Broderick did look as if he'd just seen a ghost, only this apparition was very much alive, for it was Em.

Chapter 19

*E*m waltzed into the room with her usual aplomb, and instantly homed in on Darian, taking his face between her hands and massaging his cheeks.

"Oh, honey!" she cried. "I was worried sick about you! Did the nasty spook spray you with that horrible green stuff, huh? Don't you worry about a thing, honey. Mummy is here now. Everything is going to be all right."

"Mother," said Darian, darting embarrassed glances at both Harry and Jarrett, who stood eyeing the scene with barely concealed mirth. "Mum!" he repeated a little louder, trying to extricate himself from his mother's iron grip.

"What?" she asked, not letting go. "Can't a mother be worried about her baby? Mh? Wait until you have children of your own." Only now did she notice there were others present, and instantly let go of her son's cheeks and crossed her arms. "Broderick," she snapped from between clenched teeth.

"Em," he said just as curtly.

"What are *you* doing here?"

"I was invited," he returned.

"Not by me, you weren't."

"I invited him over," said Darian. "We need to look at the case files."

"What case files? What are you talking about?"

"The murders? Remember?"

But she was too busy glowering at her ex-husband to take any notice of this, so when she asked, "Did you bring your whore as well, Broderick?" it was obvious her mind wasn't too concerned with murders or ghosts but other, more important things. Things like her husband's cheating ways.

Harry thought it wasn't really fair that Broderick should bear the brunt of Em's anger. Now would be a good time to put herself forward as a United Nations ambassador, negotiating a peace treaty between the battling parties. So she put her foot forward and opened her mouth to speak, but before she could, Broderick announced, "It's obvious I'm not welcome here, so I'll go."

"That's the wisest thing you've said all evening!"

"It's the only thing I've managed to say all evening!"

"And a good thing too, for the mere sound of your voice reminds me of the worst part of my life: those awful years we were married!"

"Now now, Mother," Darian interrupted.

"I think you should give Broderick a chance to explain," Harry said.

"Explain?" Em asked, waving her arms like an opera diva about to launch into her best aria yet. "Explain?! What is there to explain? He thought Caroline Freeby would make for a better wife than I did and when I left it turned out he was wrong. Is she still with that matador?" she asked him.

"I don't think he was a matador," grumbled Broderick, who was slowly inching closer to the exit, happy to remove himself from the sticky scene. "Wasn't he a minister?"

"Matador, minister, who cares?" she asked dramatically. "Well, you did, obviously, for in the autumn of your life you suddenly find yourself alone!"

"Look, Emmanuella," he now said, suddenly gaining courage. "Nothing ever happened between me and Caroline. All I ever did was take a few yoga lessons, because you told me to lose weight." He spread his arms. "Why would she get involved with an ugly old guy like me? That's preposterous!"

He had a point, Harry thought, but Em didn't seem to feel the same way. "You're a catch, Broderick," she said with choked voice. "You've always been a catch, only you never realized it. Caroline knew very well what she did when she seduced you. With her bendy body, and her… her yoga moves!"

"But she never did seduce me, did she?! Too busy with her minister."

"I don't believe you," she said, and that was the crux of the matter, Harry saw. She was asking Broderick to prove that something hadn't happened. It simply wasn't possible. And Broderick, the consummate policeman, knew it.

"It's no use," he said, admitting defeat. "You'll never believe me."

"No, I won't!" Em announced passionately.

And Broderick was just about to exit the scene when suddenly a loud snuffle sounded and he looked back, directing a pleading look at Em. "Oh, darling, don't cry. You know I can't stand it when you cry."

"I'm not crying," Em said huffily. "I haven't shed a single tear over you and I never will."

He frowned. "But then what…"

And then a loud sniff rent the air, and this time even Em heard it, for she said, "Oh, God, not again."

Before their eyes suddenly a little girl manifested on the carpet. She was sitting cross-legged, with bowed head, and was sobbing inconsolably.

Harry quickly directed a look at Em, and she nodded. It was the same little girl she'd seen before.

Then she looked at Broderick, and saw that his eyes had widened considerably, and his jaw was slowly dropping as he stared at the apparition.

"Hey, honey," said Harry, happy that she was finally making contact with one of the inhabitants of this apartment. "What are you crying about, mh?"

It was perhaps a dumb question, but inspiration had momentarily left her.

"My little brother…" the girl said, still sobbing and looking up at Harry with tear-filled eyes. "I can't seem to find him anywhere. Where is he?"

"Oh, I'm sure he's around here somewhere," she said soothingly. Then she held out a hand. "Do you want to go and find him together?"

The girl seemed to waver, but finally nodded, and took Harry's hand. The presence of the cold fingers slipping into hers momentarily gave her pause, but then she steeled herself, and walked with the little girl to the meditation room, where she assumed her bedroom had been before.

"What's your name, honey?" she asked softly.

"Abigail. Abigail Pringle."

"Where did you see your brother last?" she asked, the others staring on in wonder.

The little girl pointed at the room. "He was in his cradle when I went to bed, but I haven't seen him since I woke up, and the bad men came."

"So what did you do when the bad men came?"

Abigail plunked down on the floor, right on top of Em's yoga mat, which was still a bit sticky from before. "I hid," she said, then pointed at the bookcase. "Inside the wardrobe. But now it's gone. Everything's gone."

"And what did you see?"

"I—the bad men came in and they..." She swallowed as more tears trickled down her cheeks. "They came in and they had knives—very big knives. And then they must have seen me because..." She heaved a heart-wrenching sob. "They opened the wardrobe door and then..." She hiccuped. "And then they killed me," she added, almost as an afterthought.

"Did—did you get a good look at the men's faces?" she asked, sitting down next to the girl. The others now stood gathered in the doorframe, following the story intently.

Abigail shook her head, damp tresses dangling around a pale face. "They had masks. One man was very big, like a giant. The other was real thin."

"Did they say anything?" she asked. "Did they talk to you before..." She swallowed. This was hard. Much harder than it had been with Buckley. But then Buckley was a grown-up, and this was just a little girl.

Abigail now looked up at her, eyes brimming with tears. "He said it was my just reward for all that my family had done. But I told him I hadn't done anything, and he said little did I know..." She sighed. "It hurt, Miss, but only for a moment, and then it was all right again. Then it was just fine. Only now I can't find my little brother. I can't find Tanner."

"Do you think the men took him?"

The girl stared up at her, then slowly nodded. "Maybe. So do you think he's still alive?"

Harry smiled. "I'm sure that wherever he is, he's fine. And so are you. Have you seen your mum and dad?"

"They're here," she said quietly. "They're all here."

"And they've been here all his time?"

Abigail nodded, twisting her fingers.

"So why..." She bit her lip. This was starting to turn into a police interrogation, and she wondered how much more the girl could stand before freaking out and covering her in goo. "Why did you show yourself now? Why not sooner?"

The girl stared at her. "Because they're coming back."

"Who's coming back?" she asked with a frown.

"Well, the men, of course," said the girl, now frowning at her. "Don't you know anything? They're coming back, and they're going to finish the job."

She stared at her. "What do you mean?"

"They're going to make you all dead," said the girl simply, dark eyes wide. "They're going to make you all dead until there's no one left in the house."

And at this, she quickly got up and walked into the wall.

Harry wanted to ask her about a hundred other questions, but when she called out, "Hey! Abigail! Come back!" no response came.

"I'll be damned," Broderick huffed, and added, "This house is haunted!"

Chapter 20

They were all huddled around the dining room table, Broderick's file open and its contents spread across the surface of the table. It was imperative now that they determine what was going on, Harry felt, and she knew the answer had to be in this case report somewhere. Broderick had given them the gist of the report, or what he remembered anyway, and now they were poring over its pages, reading a significant part out loud here, pointing out some point of interest there, while Jarrett made copious notes of this, the first extended Wraith Wranglers meeting. Though only Harry and Jarrett were the official Wraith Wranglers present, it now seemed they'd acquired the assistance of no less than two Scotland Yardies and one policeman's wife to boot.

The house, called Brunskill Manor at the time, had welcomed the denizens of the Cromwell family from as early as the nineteen-fifties. When Anselm Pringle and Leandra Pringle, née Cromwell, had moved in, it was because they needed a place to stay for them and their five kids, and Leandra's parents, Etzel and Adele Cromwell, graciously decided to share a house that was too big for them anyway.

The only stipulation they made was that they could live out

their lives at Brunskill Manor, being taken care of by their favorite daughter. They'd occupied a sizable apartment on the top floor, while the Pringles occupied the rest of the house. Anselm's brother Jeffrey, who'd lived in what was now the Bruna Mars apartment, had moved in a little while later, jobless and penniless, and so had Anselm's little sister Cicily, who was still in college at the time, bringing the total tally up to six adults and five children.

The entire family had been home on the night of the murders, Christmas Eve 1981, except for Cicily, who'd been out with some friends, and the killers, whoever they were, had brutally slain every last inhabitant, making ten victims in all. Except, the body of Tanner Pringle, who was only a few months old, was never found. The whole thing had hit London hard, and the pressure on Broderick and his team to find the culprits had been significant.

They'd gone through the house with a fine-tooth comb, searching high and low for clues and whatnot, but unfortunately had found very little. And as far as suspects was concerned, Leandra's sister Callesta had been looked at. Apparently there had been a dispute about the house, with Callesta feeling that she'd been left empty-handed when her parents invited the Pringles to live at Brunskill Manor. The deal was that Callesta got Leandra's old apartment, as she was single and had no kids, whereas Leandra had a sizable brood. Callesta didn't feel this was fair, however.

It had created a rift in the Cromwell family that hadn't healed at the time of the murders, and both sisters hadn't spoken to each other in years.

But even though Callesta might have had motive, she also had a solid alibi, and so had her live-in boyfriend. In fact all of the surviving Pringles and Cromwells had perfect alibis, and so had Cicily Pringle. The investigation had quickly languished and the murders were never solved.

No fingerprints were ever found on the scene, nor any other evidence, as the killers had been extremely careful. The fact that all the murders had been carried out with knives had told Broderick that perhaps there was a motive of vengeance—the killers carrying out some sort of personal vendetta, and since nothing of value had been stolen, that theory had quickly gained prominence.

The whole 'Brunskill Manor Massacre' was a media frenzy, and the crime was still often mentioned as one of most baffling crimes in British history. It hadn't stopped Broderick from making a career in the Yard, even though to this day he cited the case as one of the most frustrating ones in his career.

"Not a single break," he now told the others, shaking his head. "We didn't catch a single break in this case. It was just one big baffling mystery, and one of my biggest failures. Lord knows we tried to provide justice for the Pringle and Cromwell families but unfortunately we failed miserably at our task."

"But why didn't you tell me that this entire place was a murder house?" Em asked. "You should have warned me, Broderick. I had a right to know."

"I didn't want to frighten you," grunted Broderick. "God knows it's hard enough as it is to find decent and affordable lodgings in London, let alone two adjacent units. And I knew that if you learned the full history of Brunskill Manor you'd simply refuse to move in."

"Bruna Mars told me her apartment had been the scene of a murder, and the Horrocks apartment as well, but even she didn't know the full story," said Em. "And to think I've been meditating in that room for months!"

She shuddered at the thought and Harry could see why. It is perhaps not very conducive to attaining a state of peaceful bliss and meditation five feet from the spot where a little girl was brutally murdered, especially if the ghost of that little girl insists on sticking around long after the fact.

"Still, you must have had some idea of what happened here," said Jarrett now. "Some theory perhaps? I mean, you're Scotland Yard. The cream of the crop. London's finest. The best of the best of the best and all that rot."

"All that rot is right," grumbled Broderick. "I never had a clue, to be honest. Not a single one. Oh, plenty of tips poured in when the BBC aired our request for help from the general public but none of them were actionable. There were some rumors that Anselm Pringle had racked up a considerable gambling debt, but if he had no one ever came forward to confirm or deny, and the story was quickly written off as just another rumor."

This gave Harry an idea. She'd recently had dealings with a well-known crime boss. A man who'd been around for decades, ruling London's underworld. "Perhaps you could interview Master Edwards?" she suggested.

Darian gave this some thought. "I'll see what I can do," he said reluctantly, not too keen on reacquainting himself with the criminal overlord.

"Do you really think we have to solve these murders before these ghosts will have eternal rest?" Jarrett asked. "I mean, can't we just... chat with them and ask them to move along already?"

"It doesn't work like that, Jarrett," she said. "They're only going to move on when their souls have finally found peace. And without a solution for the heinous crime that was committed against them that is not going to happen."

"Did you ever find the body of the brother?" asked Darian. "Tanner?"

"No, we did not," replied his father, absently rubbing his buzz cut. He seemed tense, all of a sudden, which wasn't surprising, as he'd just described this case as one of the biggest failure of his career.

"I wonder what happened to him," said Darian.

"Me too," Harry chimed in. "He was just a baby."

Broderick cleared his throat noisily. "Look, why don't we call it a night," he now suggested. "It's late and frankly I'm tired."

"I don't want to stay here alone," said Em, returning to a favorite theme.

"I'll stay with you," Harry assured her. "No way I'm leaving you alone."

"Me too," said Jarrett, stretching. "We can have a slumber party!"

"I'm going home," said Broderick, after a wistful glance at his ex-wife.

"I think that's for the best," she said, shattering his hopes of some form of reunion.

"And I'm going back to my apartment," said Darian. He clapped his father on the back. "You're welcome to stay at my place. What do you say?"

"No, thanks," Broderick said, a deep frown etched on his brow. "Your apartment is quite possibly the gloomiest place on earth. I'd rather stay at the Tower of London."

"What is it with you guys and my apartment?!" cried Darian, dismayed.

"We all have taste, darling," Em pointed out, "and you do not."

At this, Darian was the first to rise to his feet. "Suit yourself," he said with a shrug. "But next time you start screaming your head off when you see the ghost of Abigail Pringle I won't come running. I'll be sound asleep!"

"So what's the plan?" Harry asked, stifling a cavernous yawn.

"Darian is going to have a little chat with Master Edwards," Jarrett reminded her. "See if he knows about Anselm Pringle's secret criminal past."

"Right. And we're going to try and talk to more ghosts," said Harry. "See if we can't jog their memories. One of them must have seen something."

Broderick stared at her. "You know, that's quite amazing."

"What is?" she asked, now really yearning for a soft bed. She had the distinct impression that tonight she wasn't going to have trouble sleeping.

"That you can talk to the victims. I'll bet you can solve a lot of crimes."

"That's the whole point, Mr. Watley. That's why we do it, isn't it, Jer?"

"Well, we also do it because we love hanging out with ghouls of all shapes and sizes—and color of mucus—but yes, solving crimes is a big part of it."

"That's amazing," he rumbled. "And helpful. If only I'd known about this before, we could have solved a lot of crimes together, Miss McCabre." He glanced at his son. "Are you listening, Darian? You have to work with these Wraith Wranglers. They're the next big thing in law enforcement, you hear?"

Darian merely shook his head. He didn't seem to see eye to eye with his father on this.

"I'm glad you're finally beginning to see the light, Broderick," said Em. "Now if only you'd see the light on that little yoga teacher of yours..."

The chief inspector's frown made an instant comeback. "I told you, Emmanuella, I never so much as laid a finger on..."

But Em held up a hand, like a traffic cop. "Save it for the jury, Broderick. I'm not interested." She turned to Harry. "Harry? Are you coming? Time for bed and for these two stubborn coppers to leave this premises."

These last words were spoken with a withering look at her ex-husband, who got the message, apparently, for he now quickly proceeded to the exit.

"You have to do something with this, Darian," Harry heard Broderick insist. "These Wraith Wranglers? They can be a real boon to any investigation, you know? A real boon."

"I know, Dad," said Darian resignedly. "I know."

Chapter 21

*J*arrett couldn't sleep. He'd been tossing and turning for what seemed like hours. It was a rare experience. Like he'd told Harry, he usually slept like a baby. Better even, for babies often had a lot on their minds, like when to get their next meals, and he never had anything on his mind. Critics would have said he didn't have much of a mind to begin with, but haters will be haters.

Em had given him the spare bedroom, while she and Harry occupied the main bedroom, and he was already regretting having agreed to stay over.

For one thing, the room was literally littered with small figurines of an erotic nature which he was finding oddly disturbing, and for another, the curtains allowed a lot of light from the street lamps to filter into the room, and he'd forgotten to bring his trusty sleep mask.

He groaned in agony, and finally, after performing another turn, like a chicken on a grill, he kicked away the bed sheets with an annoyed grunt and crawled out of bed. Even though he'd extolled the virtues of taking sleeping pills to Harry, he decided that what the doctor ordered was a glass of warm milk and some honey. Like his sleep mask, he'd left his sleeping pills at home, and he wasn't prepared to bother Deshawn in the middle of the night.

So he sauntered into the kitchen, found the milk in the fridge, a pot in the cupboard over the sink and the honey beneath it and started the process of warming himself up some of the heavenly white brew.

The living room was dark, the only light provided by the lamp beneath the cupboard, which was ample for his purposes. And as he sat there, sipping from the restorative, he thought he saw a shimmer on the living room wall.

He blinked, figuring his eyes were playing tricks on him, but then the shimmer became more pronounced, and a chill settled around his heart.

The shimmer had appeared at the exact same spot where Darian's attacker had lunged at him earlier that evening. And as he watched with bated breath, he felt a cold shiver running down his spine, in spite of the warm milk glugging down his gullet. He quickly put down his cup and braced himself, his hands gripping the kitchen counter feverishly.

Before his frightened eyes, the ghost of the woman who'd attacked Darian now came drifting from the wall. First her face became visible, the spitting image of Em's face, but this one twisted in agony, her long raven hair covered by a sort of veil. And then the rest of her swirled from the wall, like wisps of mist wafting up over a field, quickly removing the world from sight.

She seemed sad and lost, as her face displayed her extreme sorrow. She seemed to be looking for something as she hovered here and there. Jarrett, now perfectly still, didn't even dare to breathe as he stared at the apparition. He might be one of the fearless Wraith Wranglers, but he was scared stiff.

Oh, crap, he thought. Crapperdicrapperdicrapperdicrap. He just hoped the ghost of the late Pringle matriarch wouldn't see him and would just disappear into her wall soon. Nice ghost, he thought. Nice ghosty ghosty.

But then his pinky finger accidentally displaced the teaspoon and it clattered against the plate. Yikes! The ghost instantly looked up in dismay, her dark eyes locking on his, and he could see her face opening up like a large ferryboat, about to distribute some of her trademark green goo, so he ducked beneath the counter, not wanting to be there when the sticky stuff hit!

But instead of covering the kitchen with slime, nothing happened! And when he popped his head back up, he found himself face to face with her!

"Aaaargh!" he cried eloquently, jerking back. "Aaaaaargh!" he repeated for good measure, eyes wide and feeling the chill emanating from her.

"Where is my son?" she asked in a voice that seemed to travel through water. "Where is my little boy?"

"I—I'm sure I don't know!" he cried.

"They took him from me. They took them all. And now he's coming back. And so are they. Can't you hear it?" she asked, rearing up. "They're coming!"

"No, I can't hear a thing," he confessed, his teeth chattering wildly.

"Tanner is returning," she warbled, eyes roving. "But not yet. Not yet."

"That—that's great!" he said, trying to produce a careless laugh but only managing to make a coughing sound. "I'm so happy for you, Mrs. Pringle!"

Then he remembered he was a Wraith Wrangler now, and should probably try and solve the mystery of these murders, just like they'd agreed. So he swallowed with some difficulty, gathered his courage, and addressed the woman again. "I, um, Mrs. Pringle? Mind if I ask you a question?"

The woman, who'd been sniffing at his cup of warm milk,

turned her dark eyes on him again. "Yes?"

"Um, could you please tell me… The men who killed you, do you have any idea who they were? I mean, it would help me greatly if—it would help you greatly if—it would help the present owners of this apartment greatly if—"

"They wore masks," she interrupted him. "Both of them. One was tall and thin, the other large and muscular, so I have no idea who they were."

"But why…" He swallowed again, the intense scrutiny she was awarding him now wreaking havoc on his nervous system. If he'd thought coming out here was going to make him sleep better he'd been sorely mistaken. "Why did they do this? Why murder your family?" he asked the obvious question.

"I don't know, young man. I've been asking myself the same question for thirty years—or is it fifty? It's so easy to lose count after so many years."

"Did you have any enemies? Anyone who would mean you harm?"

"Only my sister," she said acerbically. "But even Callesta would never be mean enough to do something like this. She'd never want to hurt her own."

"Yes, I can see what you mean," he said, then latched onto another idea. "Perhaps they were your husband's associates? A deal gone wrong?"

"Anselm swears this wasn't his doing." She spread her arms, wisps of fog wafting from them. The whole thing was actually quite beautiful to watch, he thought, but also downright spooky. "When we married he promised me that all his gambling and drinking were a thing of the past. And I believe him."

"Did you have any… valuables that were stolen? Perhaps that's what they were after? Jewels or, um, half a million pounds in the family safe?"

"We were never rich. Not by any means. This house belonged to my parents, but that was as far as our wealth went. Anselm was a plumber, and a solid earner, but only barely enough to provide for a family of seven."

"And your parents? Perhaps they had some money stashed away?"

"All they had was Brunskill Manor, which they inherited from my grandparents. The Cromwells were never rich and neither were the Pringles."

"Such a mystery," he murmured, and Leandra Pringle agreed that the whole thing was baffling to a degree.

"But the thing that vexes me the most is that they took my little boy."

"They took him? They didn't... I mean, they didn't, well, murder him?"

"A mother knows, sir. No, Tanner is still alive. I can feel it."

"But then he must be..." He did a quick calculation in his head, which took him longer than it probably should have. "He must be thirty-five now."

She was staring at him dreamily now. "I can feel him. He's coming back."

"When is that, exactly? Any idea?"

"Soon," said the woman, and her face blossomed into a chilly smile. "Soon we'll all be reunited again. One big, happy family once more."

The word 'reunited' gave him pause. "Wait, do you mean he's coming back here to die?"

She gave him a cold stare. "No, sir. Tanner is coming back here to kill."

Chapter 22

Darian didn't like the particular assignment Harry had saddled him up with. Having a chat with Master Edwards wasn't exactly his favorite pastime. But he could see she had a point. If anyone knew what happened in the London underworld in the eighties it most definitely was Bill Edwards, once the undisputed leader of that underworld himself, and perhaps to this day.

The man lived in a sizable mansion in the East End, at the end of a short cul-de-sac in a gated community. The house that a lot of crime money had built. And even though these days Edwards claimed he was a reformed crook, Darian had his doubts. A man like him had crime in his blood.

When he called to set up the meeting, Edwards had been most courteous and actually seemed to look forward to this social call, as he called it.

Once seated in front of the man in his ornate office, where probably numerous elements of the criminal classes had once stood before him, he let a curious eye slide across the hallmarks of a long and prosperous career.

Edwards was seated behind a mahogany desk, the centerpiece

of the room, heavy drapes half closed and preventing what little light there was in the London skies to creep into the room. He stared at the former crook, a majestic figure, looking resplendent now in a burgundy housecoat. For some reason he reminded him of Hugh Hefner, the owner of the sprawling Playboy mansion. The two men shared the same facial features, and the same ageless quality, even though Edwards was probably the same age as Hefner.

"Darian Watley as I live and breathe," he now said as a pleasant grin spread across his wrinkly features. "To what do I owe the honor, Inspector?"

"Well..." He hesitated, wondering how to launch into this. "The thing is... I've been assigned a cold case, and was hoping you might be able to shed some light on it," he said, deciding not to mention the entire ghost angle.

"A cold case, huh? I love those!" cried the reformed criminal.

Both men looked up when the door opened and a large man with no neck to speak of strode in carrying a silver salver with a cup of tea and biscuits.

Darian frowned darkly when he recognized the man as Philo Bovine-Marks, one of Edwards's goons. He'd once arrested him himself, for trying to murder Harry, and he wasn't happy that he'd made parole.

"Hello, Inspector Watley. Looking good, sir," he said pleasantly.

"Wish I could say the same about you," he said acerbically.

"How's Harry McCabre, by the way? Still perky?" asked Philo with a wide grin, and anger flared in Darian's eyes before he could control himself.

"Easy now, Inspector," chuckled Edwards, who'd recognized the signs. "No need to get all worked up. We're civilized people here, aren't we, Philo?"

"Oh, yes, sir," said Philo, still with that same stupid grin on his smug mug. "We're totally legit now, Inspector Watley. Completely on the up and up."

"You bet. I've been given a new lease on life, Darian, and I intend to use it to create some good. So your little girlfriend is quite safe, isn't she, Philo?"

"Oh, yes, sir. Quite safe indeed. I wouldn't harm a hair on that cute little blond head of hers. No way." And as he left the room, after pouring Darian a cup of Earl Grey, he added, "Give her my best regards, Inspector. And please tell her that when I tried to kill her it was never personal. Simply business."

He gritted his teeth as the big guy waddled out, and shook his head. "For a man who professes to have changed his life around you seem to keep to the same bad company you always have, Edwards."

"You mean Philo? Oh, but he's such a dear old friend. Has been with me for more years than I care to remember. And you can see he's adapted to the new regime quite well."

"Yeah, he's gone from dispensing bullets to dispensing tea," he grumbled.

Edwards laughed. "Honestly, Inspector, I wouldn't know what to do without him."

"I would," he said through gritted teeth.

Edwards wagged a reproachful finger. "Vengeance is a very nasty emotion, Inspector. I, for one, have learned to forgive and forget. It's the only way to live! You can't abide anger in your heart. It will give you heartburn. And now on to your cold case. Tell me all about it," he said, steepling his fingers on the desk and cocking his head like a parrot, ready to listen.

He sighed. "You may have heard of the Brunskill Manor Massacre?" And as he launched into the story of what happened that fateful night thirty-five years ago, he was gratified to see that Edwards was riveted, only interrupting him from time to time to ask clarification on some minor detail here or there, listening intently all the while. And when finally he wrapped up the story, Edwards remained perfectly still for a moment, lips pursed in thought.

"I remember the Brunskill Manor Massacre," he said. "A dozen members of the same family, all murdered in one single night. A genuine tragedy."

"There were rumors that Anselm Pringle was involved with some unsavory characters," Darian said. "That he owed a lot of people money."

"And you thought about me?" asked Edwards now, visibly offended.

Darian shrugged. "There was talk about gambling debts. Big tabs."

Edwards nodded. "Yes, before I had a change of heart, I was indeed something of a big shot in that world. But if Anselm Pringle owed anybody any money, it wasn't me. And I certainly never heard of any of my former associates or even competitors ever ordering the man's entire family murdered. Thinking back though," he said, leaning back in his chair, "I must confess that one aspect of the story has stuck with me. The disappearance of the youngest son of the Pringles. His body was never found, you say?"

"No, it wasn't. So either he was murdered and his body disposed of, or..."

"He's still alive," said Edwards, his keen eyes flickering. Then he grinned. "If he were still alive, he'd be thirty-five today. Isn't that your age, Darian?"

"Yes," said Darian, "but I don't see how that's relevant."

"You could be the Pringle kid, and not even be aware of it."

Darian didn't think this was funny. "Look, my age has got nothing to do with this."

"What I mean to say is, the kid could have been snatched and placed in another home. He wouldn't have a clue as he was only a toddler at the time." His eyes were flickering dangerously now. "How much do you remember?"

"From when I was a baby? Nothing." This entire conversation was starting to annoy him. "What are you saying, Edwards? That you know where Tanner Pringle is?"

Edwards lifted his hands. "I'm not saying anything, Inspector. But perhaps to solve this mystery you should try and find Tanner. Because when you find him you might also find whoever killed his family, and perhaps even the whole reason behind the Brunskill Manor Massacre."

"What?" he asked with a laugh. "You want me to wrangle up all of London's thirty-five-year-old males? There must be thousands!"

"Not *all* the thirty-five-year-olds, Inspector. Just Tanner Pringle."

He made a gesture of annoyance. "Look, Edwards, if you know where the Pringle kid is, just tell me already, will you? I'm not in the mood for games."

A smile played about the crime boss's lips, as if he was having a blast. Then he asked softly, "Do you want to know where Tanner is, Darian?"

"Yes, I do, dammit!" he cried.

Edwards grinned evilly. "I'm looking right at him."

Chapter 23

"What do you think you're doing?" Jarrett muttered with sleepy voice.

Harry had just opened the curtains with a vigorous flick of the wrist, and sun was streaming into the guest room he occupied. "Rise and shine, sleepyhead!" she caroled. "You're wasting the best part of the day."

"Oh, God, lemme sleep..." was his eloquent response.

"It's nine o'clock," she said primly. "You should be up and about." And with those horrible words, she started to drag the sheet from his sleepy form.

"You're just like my mother," he lamented. "Every single morning she would drag me out of bed, with some specious excuse about school."

"Well, for your information I'm not your mother, Jarrett, but I do have a Tube train to catch to work, and you have ghosts to catch."

He tried to pull the sheet over his eyes again, but to no avail. Harry was a lot stronger than she looked, and yanked the sheet clean off the bed, leaving him unprotected from the light. "Gah!" he grunted when a straying ray of sunshine hit his eyes and he quickly held up a hand in protection.

"You're like a vampire," she said with a light laugh. "Afraid of the light."

"I was up half the night chatting with Leandra Pringle, for your information," he grumbled as he assumed an upright position and propped the pillow behind his back. "So excuse me for not leaping from the bed with a cheerful song on my lips and a pleasant smile on my face."

She gasped, as he knew she would. "Leandra? You saw Leandra?"

He yawned. "I couldn't sleep so I went to prepare myself a glass of warm milk and she popped out of the wall and we had a nice little chat."

Harry plopped down on the bed. "And what did she have to say?"

"Well..." He frowned, trying to remember the conversation. "Apparently she seems to feel that her boy... um, Tanner? Well, he's coming back."

"Oh, my God. That means he's still alive!"

"Yep, and she also mentioned he's coming back... to kill."

"Kill?" Harry's eyes went wide. "Kill who? Kill why? Kill when? Kill how?"

He rubbed his eyes. "So many questions on an empty stomach," he lamented. "Can we save the third degree for after breakfast?"

"No, we can't save the third degree for after breakfast," she said, getting up. "I have to get going. The customers of Buckley's Antiques won't wait."

"Why don't you just, you know, get a manager to run the store for you?"

"Can't do it," she said, shaking her head. "I'm not exactly running a Starbucks, Jarrett. It's a boutique antique store, and rarely turns a profit."

"So sell it. You don't even like antiques." Or know very much about it, he wanted to add, but managed to bite his tongue just in time.

"I do like antiques," she said, piqued. "And I love running my own store."

"Suit yourself. But if you'd like I could buy you." He directed a more or less clear-focused look at her. In the morning his vision was always a little blurry. "And then we could finally do this wraith wrangling thing the way it should be done: as equal partners in an actual business venture."

She was frowning at him, he saw. "You would do that?"

"In a heartbeat," he assured her. "But not before breakfast, of course."

She chewed her bottom lip, then shook her head, her blond locks swirling around her pixie face. "I don't know. We'd have to ask Brian. The Wraith Wranglers are his concept. We're like... his franchisees or something."

"You can't be a franchisee if nobody's paying you," he pointed out.

"No, but you know what I mean."

He did know what she meant, and it irked him that Harry had to find ways to support herself while Brian Rutherford was sitting on a mountain of money. The heir to the Wardop fortune was adamant to keep the Wraith Wranglers organization a volunteer thing, and refused to pay Harry or Jarrett for their services, or to demand remuneration from their clients.

"Let's found this wraith wrangling thing on sound footing," he suggested. "And let's be equal partners in the venture. Actual business partners."

She seemed to waver. "I don't know, Jarrett. I made a promise to Buckley I would take good care of his store for him. I can't just break that promise."

"You would be taking good care of it," he pointed out. "If I bought the store I'd simply hire a manager to run it. And us Zephyrs always get value for our money. It would be the best manager money could buy. Someone who knows their antiques. I'm sure Buckley would understand that you can't be at the store and be a wraith wrangler at the same time. Honestly, how are you going to wrangle wraiths when you're stuck at the store all the time?"

"I know," she said with a sigh.

"And what's more, you're not even doing great business."

She groaned. "You don't have to remind me. I feel terrible about that."

He patted her knee. "You sell the store to me, and with that money you buy yourself a fifty percent share in our very own wraith wrangling business. And then you'll finally be doing what you were always meant to do, honey."

She looked up. "You think so? Wrangling wraiths is my destiny?"

"I'm sure of it. No one wrangles wraiths like you do."

"But you did so well with Leandra Pringle last night."

"Oh, that," he said deferentially. "To be honest I had no idea what I was doing." Which was, of course, the story of his life. He never knew what he was doing. Not that that ever stopped him. "And now if you'll excuse me," he said, getting up, "it's time for my morning toilette, followed by a much-needed brekkie. All this ghost wrangling has given me a considerable appetite."

"And I'm going to open up the store," she said, then paused in the doorframe. "You know, this might not be such a bad idea, Jarrett?"

"It's a great idea. And don't worry about Brian. I'm sure he'll be more than happy when we foot the occasional expense bill ourselves. If he's like any other billionaire I know, the more pennies he can pinch, the better."

Chapter 24

When Harry finally left, Jarrett briefly considered going back to bed and putting in a few more hours of sleep. But then he figured that since he was up already, he might just as well start his day. The words of Leandra Pringle had worried him a great deal, and so had those of her daughter. As he interpreted them, the ones responsible for the Brunskill Manor Massacre had decided to play a return date, and Tanner Pringle was going to be waiting for them when they did, determined to take revenge for the murder of his family.

And since he didn't think it was a good idea for anyone to be present at the re-enactment of the climactic scene of High Noon, he decided to tell Em to join the others at the Ritz, and not spend another night at her haunted home. But when he walked into the living room, he found the apartment empty, his hostess with the mostess conspicuously absent. And then he found a little note she'd put up on the fridge: 'Gone to the hair salon. Back at noon. Em.'

After a vigorous frothing in the shower, and an equally bracing breakfast, he was on the phone with Deshawn, getting a sit rep on the state of affairs at the Ritz. He was gratified to hear that his guests had enjoyed a splendid night. He hated to inform his manservant that Brunskill Manor still wasn't safe for human habitation, and that the ghosts hadn't been turned from the door yet. And that it behooved the Marses and the Horrockses to postpone their return to their respective homesteads for just a little while longer.

And as he was giving Deshawn some further instructions, he began to wonder if putting up these unfortunate homeowners was quite enough. Perhaps there was more he could do—more people he could evacuate?

Brunskill Manor consisted of nine apartments, and Em had told him that two were currently vacant, one occupant was away on business and one on holiday in Turks and Caicos, which left one owner or tenant unaccounted for.

And as this happened to be the one bunking on the top floor, where Etzel and Adele Cromwell had lived, things weren't boding well for that person. Em had never met the current occupant of the apartment, who apparently was the reticent type, and liked to keep very much to him or herself. Putting down his phone—and a forkful of scrambled eggs—he wondered if he shouldn't warn them that Brunskill Manor was about to become the scene of another massacre. Or perhaps he shouldn't invade their precious privacy?

But then he steeled himself to the task, reminding himself he was now a full-fledged wraith wrangler, and was soon pushing the button to rise one floor. He could have taken the stairs, of course, but since he'd already made himself breakfast, and was about to embark on a rescue mission, he figured he shouldn't overtax himself. Besides, someone had to pay his respects to the descendants of Prince Leopold from *Kate & Leopold* fame, who was, after all, the official inventor of the Otis elevators. He'd always loved that movie.

And he was still contemplating the many virtues of Hugh

Jackman when he pressed his finger on the doorbell to apartment number 9.

He didn't know what he'd expected, but it definitely wasn't this. The occupant, when he finally answered the door, turned out to be a hunk of a man, standing a full head taller than Jarrett himself, at least fourteen stone. The man was colossal, dressed in a fashionably ripped pink tank top and flimsy mint green boxer shorts, wiping his smoothly shaved head with a towel.

For a brief moment, he simply gawked, then finally hitched up his jaw, and said, "I, um..." He hadn't actually prepared an opening statement, and now realized his faux-pas. So, as usual, he simply said the first thing that popped into his head. "Have you seen a ghost, sir?"

The man mountain eyed him curiously. "A what?"

"A ghost," he clarified. "Or ghosts, plural," he added, still trying to wrap his head around so much male beauty standing only a few inches away from him. "An elderly couple to be precise? They used to live here," he explained, starting to realize how strange his visit must seem to the untrained eye.

The man's eyes, which were set a little too closely together and were green, narrowed. "An elderly ghost couple?"

"Yes, exactly," he said, well pleased that his message was at least coming across loud and clear. "Have you seen them by any chance?"

"Why? Are they missing?" he asked.

"Oh, no," he said with a short laugh. His eyes now drifted from the man's classically handsome face to his corded shoulders to his bulging pecs and then down to what he could only surmise was a very solid six-pack. "Wow," he couldn't help but mutter. "Do you work out, by any chance, Mr..."

"Flax. Thorley Flax." He grinned. "Yeah, I so work out, buddy.

In fact I was in the middle of my second workout of the day when you rang my bell."

"I work out, too," said Jarrett, "but obviously not as passionately as you."

"Do you want to see my equipment?" suddenly asked the man.

"Of course," he said after a pause. "I would love to see your equipment."

"Step right in," said Mr. Flax, stepping aside so Jarrett could step in. "Who are you, by the way?" he asked as he led the way through the hallway and into a second bedroom turned into a very nicely appointed home gym.

"Jarrett Zephyr-Thornton the Third," he said automatically as his eyes took in the high-end fitness equipment. A huge flatscreen TV was playing an episode of CHiPs, while Duran Duran was pumping through the speakers and a second TV screen displayed a soccer game. The cacophony was overwhelming and ear-splitting, and he raised his voice to ask, "This room looks like the den of an Olympian. Are you an Olympian, Mr. Flax?"

The big guy laughed. "Nope, I'm just a Chippendale, buddy."

"Ah, oh, ooh," said Jarrett, gulping slightly. He hadn't expected this.

"And please call me Thorley... Jarrett, is it? You know, your face looks kinda familiar. Have we met? Passed each other in the vestibule maybe?"

"No, I don't live here," he said, then his eye caught a third TV set, where an episode of Celebrity Big Brother was playing. He pointed at it. "You may have seen me on there. I did CBB two seasons ago?"

Thorley now pointed a finger at him, a wide smile creasing his face. "Of course! I remember you! You were kicked out of the house so fast they called you the most unpopular candidate ever!

Richest man in England, right?"

"Well, actually that honor is reserved for my father, but let's not split, um heirs, if you catch my drift."

"Zephyr. Of course. And now you're in the ghost hunting business, huh? I saw an ad in the paper the other day. Wraith wrestling? Are you for real?"

"Wraith wrangling, and yes, I'm very much for real," he said, watching as Thorley plunked his impressive glutes down on the seat of a back training machine, took a firm hold of the handles and started shifting a block of weights up and down the size of the Empire State Building, or so it seemed.

Jarrett's eyes were riveted on the undulating muscles of Thorley's upper back, moving beneath his bronzed skin, and he gulped a little. It's one thing to enjoy the fine men of the Chippendales on stage, but quite another to see one up close and personal. It was like watching Magic Mike, but for real.

"You know," shouted Thorley between two grunts as he pulled down the stacked weights, "the previous owner did warn me about some strange noises in the place. But to be honest... I never noticed anything out of the ordinary."

Jarrett eyed the blaring TV, the second blaring TV, the third blaring TV, drowned out by the blaring radio, and figured that ghosts would have to shout really hard to make themselves heard over all this racket. And since this was an elderly couple, they'd probably gone into hiding now that their lodgings had been taken over by this extremely vociferous bodybuilder.

"Well, if you do happen to see them, don't hesitate to get in touch," he shouted, placing his business card on a small side table fully laden with bulky containers of protein powder and very large bottles of energy drinks.

"Oh, hey, that's great, buddy," said the guy. "Will do. Say, and if you want to work out sometime, just holler. I can always use a spotter." And at this, he put in his final rep, with a loud animal cry, his muscles bulging and his veins throbbing dangerously, and then he let go of the stack, which clattered into place again, and got up, toweling his face and shaved head.

"Oh, yes," he said. "Yes, of course. If you need a spotter, I'm your man. No doubt about it." He was suddenly feeling very hot under the collar.

The colossus grinned and took his hand in his own, sweaty paw. "Jarrett Zephyr-Thornton the Third. This is so cool, man! I never thought I'd ever meet an actual real-life celebrity. It's an honor, Jarrett. A real honor."

"Oh, but the honor is all mine," he said. "All mine," he repeated as the other man bumped his pecs against his own, more moderate specimens.

Then, quite unexpectedly, Thorley took him in a very sweaty bear hug, and whispered, "They're listening to every word we're saying, Jarrett. Now pretend I told you a joke. A great joke!" And he promptly released him.

"Ha ha!" laughed Jarrett, eyes widening in shock. "Ha ha!" he repeated.

"Funny, huh?!" Thorley asked, shaking with laughter now.

"Hilarious!" he conceded.

Then Thorley took him in a close embrace once more, which did much to raise his blood pressure to dangerous levels, and whispered, "Meet me outside in five."

"Ha ha!" boomed Jarrett, and was still laughing when Thorley showed him to the door and bade him goodbye with a wink.

Chapter 25

Harry, as she took the Tube to work, thought about Jarrett's words. Dump Buckley Antiques and start a genuine Wraith Wranglers company? Help ghosts and be paid for a change? It sounded too good to be true! On the other hand, like she'd told Jarrett, she'd promised Buckley to take care of the store, and couldn't simply break her promise now. The man had worked so hard to build his business. Could she simply sell it? Wouldn't that be a lack of respect for his legacy? Then again, it wasn't the store so much as Buckley's fencing that had made him money: he didn't balk at trading stolen antiques for big bucks, using the store that carried his name simply as a front.

Even Darian had said Buckley was more known as a high-end fence than as an antique dealer. She sighed as she held onto the bar when the Tube train bucked and shook, diving into a particularly narrow tunnel. The truth was that she would love to be more involved with the Wraith Wranglers. She felt that that was where her heart lay. Not the world of antiques. This offer by Jarrett was a very generous one, to be filed in the category of offers she couldn't possibly refuse. Still, she felt conflicted. Buckley had been more than an employer. He was her friend, and when Harry made a promise to a friend, she didn't let them down.

"Oh, Buckley," she muttered. "If only you were still around..."

She got off at the Notting Hill station and walked the short distance to the store. Overnight, someone had sprayed graffiti on the storefront's roll-down security shutters and she shook her head in dismay. She bent down to open the padlock and shoved up the shutters, revealing the store's facade. Even though she was late in arriving, there were no customers anxiously lining up outside, and if she were absolutely honest she had to admit Jarrett was right: the store was barely solvent. Now that the under-the-counter part of the business had ceased with Buckley's demise, she hardly sold a thing.

She'd used the money Buckley left her to pay off some of his debts, and part of the mortgage, and pretty much the only income Buckley Antiques now generated came from the tenant who lived above the store. And even that was a mere pittance compared to the cost of doing business.

She stepped inside and flipped the sign from Closed to Open and walked to the back, where the small safe was located in what had been Buckley's office. She opened the safe and took out the money for the cash register with a hopeful heart, as she did every morning, and walked to the counter, ready for another day.

And as she tidied up the store, her thoughts invariably turned to Darian. She was glad he'd finally seen the light—or Leandra Pringle to be exact. Now that both he and Broderick believed in ghosts, it would make her life much easier. The more people in her close circle of friends believed in ghosts, the better. Darian's skepticism had troubled her, even driven them apart. Whether this change of heart would bring them closer together again remained to be seen, but at least his interview with Master Edwards showed he was prepared to do his part in making Brunskill Manor ghost-free again.

She idly toyed with her phone for a moment, wondering whether to call Darian now, and ask him how the interview had gone, but finally decided against it. She didn't want to come across as pushy or needy. If he wanted to share his story with her he would call her in due time.

And she was just staring at a particularly unpleasant wooden sculpture of an Indian fertility symbol, when a soft cough sounded behind her. She whirled around, not having noticed any customers entering the store, and when she saw it wasn't a customer but Sir Geoffrey Buckley, she cried out, "Buckley!" and leaped straight into the old ghost's arms.

He laughed heartily. "Harry, easy now, easy now! Harry!"

"Why?" she asked, stepping back to take a good look at him. "It's not as if your old bones are liable to break or anything. Let me look at you. Oh, my—you look wonderful, Buckley!" And he did. His cheeks were actually rosy, which was exceptional for a ghost, and his eyes twinkled with delight. He was a dapper little gentleman, with frizzy gray hair and the kindly face of a hobbit. "You came back!" she cried happily.

"Oh, yes I did," he said with a grin. "Couldn't stay away now could I?"

"But how? I thought all your business here was finished?"

"Not by a long shot!" he said, chuckling delightedly. "For one thing, I see you're having quite a bit of trouble with the store, and then there's all this wraith wrangling to take into consideration." He puffed out his Savile Row-clad chest. "I'll have you know that you may now count me amongst your assistants for wrangling wraiths. If you will have me, that is, of course."

"Buckley!" she gasped. "You can't be serious?!"

"Oh, yes I am," he assured her. "I've been granted special permission to linger on this shore for as long as I see fit. To aid and abet you in aiding and abetting others like me to reach the other shore." He smiled. "Oh, Harry. I've missed you terribly!"

"And I you," she assured him, then remembered his earlier words and hesitantly asked, "How did you know the store was in trouble?"

"Hard not to. I've been watching you from afar all this time." His twinkling smile disappeared. "I'm so sorry for saddling you with this burden, Harry. If only I'd known I'd never have gifted you Buckley Antiques."

"And I'm sorry for disappointing you. I know I should have done a much better job. But with your help we'll turn this ship around again, I'm sure."

"No," he said decidedly. "The only reason I did well was because I was a crook. Now that you made the business legit there's no money to be made. I discovered a long time ago antiques is not big business, Harry. Far from it."

"I've paid off most of your debts," she said, "with the money you left me. So at least the business is pretty much debt-free now. Ready for a new start."

"If I were you I'd accept Jarrett's offer and sell the store. Someone might be able to turn it around but that someone," he quickly added when she made to speak, "is not you, unfortunately, Harry. Watching you struggle made me realize that your mission in life isn't selling antiques but helping ghosts."

"You really think so?" she asked hopefully.

"I know so," he said, placing a fatherly hand on her shoulder. "I hereby give you permission to sell Buckley Antiques to the highest bidder, Harry."

"To Jarrett. He'll add the store to the Zephyr portfolio of businesses."

"Well, the Zephyrs have the golden touch. Perhaps he can

make something of it."

"I think what he really wants is the location," she said hesitantly. "Notting Hill real estate is prime real estate. It wouldn't surprise me if he tore down the entire building and erected some luxury apartment complex in its stead."

"Then let him!" cried Buckley. "What do you care what happens to the store? Let him do whatever he wants with it."

"But it's your store, Buckley," she said. "Your life's work."

He shook his head. "That part of my life is over, Harry. Time to move on."

"Are you sure you don't mind?"

"Of course not. In fact I think it's a splendid idea! New horizons! New adventures!" He eyed her fondly. "I, for one, would love to be the silent partner in your new venture, Harry." He winked. "Your ghost partner."

She laughed. "A ghost joining a ghost helping business. It's perfect!"

"Well, run it by Jarrett and see what he says. I just hope he agrees."

She took his hand and shook it warmly. "I don't care what Jarrett says. You are welcome as the third wraith wrangler, Buckley."

He smiled, his eyes flickering with gaiety. "We'll be like the three musketeers! This calls for a celebration, Harry, only..." He faltered, and his face fell. "I fear we should postpone popping that bot of champagne, and not just because I can't drink champagne any longer. I'm afraid that our first assignment together is a tough one."

She nodded. "I know. The Brunskill Manor Massacre. I have a feeling that if we don't solve this case quickly, more terrible things are going to happen, Buckley." She sighed. "Oh, I'm so happy you're here. Perhaps you can talk to these ghosts. They've proved very reluctant to trust either me or Jarrett. At least last night Jarrett got Leandra Pringle to open up a little."

"I know," he said, and when she eyed him curiously, he added, "I've been following the case with great interest, but couldn't show myself until now, when finally I was granted permission to linger on this shore a little longer."

"Thank God," she said with feeling.

"Exactly right," he said with a chuckle. "You've placed your praise at the right door, Harry."

Her eyes went wide. "You... you met your maker? And Saint Peter and all those other guys? The pearly gates?"

"I did." He chuckled again. "I've seen it all, Harry, and I have to tell you that when you breathe your last breath, you needn't fear a thing, honey. The beyond is even more magnificent than you can imagine. A real benediction."

"Good to know, though I'm not ready to leave this world just yet."

"I know you're not. And a good thing, too. For you have many things to accomplish, Harry. A great destiny awaits you," he said seriously. "A great destiny indeed. And it is my honor and privilege to help you accomplish it."

She stared at him, more than a little flustered. "I'll take your word for it."

"Please do!" He clapped his hands. "And now let's close up this dreary old shop and get to work, shall we? Brunskill Manor waits for no one!"

Chapter 26

"But that's impossible!" Darian cried.

Master Edwards produced a fat chuckle. "I'm afraid it is possible, Darian. In fact it's absolutely true! You are Tanner Pringle. No doubt about it."

"But how can I be Tanner Pringle?" he asked, gesticulating wildly now. He'd jumped up from his chair and was pacing the study furiously, like a caged gorilla. "I'm the son of Broderick and Emmanuella Watley!"

"No, you're not," said Edwards calmly. "You were born the son of Anselm and Leandra Pringle. When you were a baby your family was massacred by an assailant or assailants unknown, and apparently snapped up for adoption by Chief Inspector Broderick Watley of Scotland Yard."

"I don't believe you," he snapped, eyeing the other man furiously. If eyes could kill Master Edwards would be a dead man right now.

But the reformed master crook didn't seem perturbed in the least. He held up his hands with a wide grin. "Don't shoot the messenger, Watley!"

Darian approached the desk and planted his hands on it,

bringing his face level with the crime lord's. "You're lying. You're simply doing this to get back at me for putting Philo in jail and making your life miserable when you were still running your nasty little crime syndicate!"

"Believe whatever you want to believe, Watley. It's no skin off my nose."

He was very much inclined to take more than some skin off the other man's nose, but managed to restrain himself with a powerful effort. "I think I would know if I were adopted. My parents would have told me."

Edwards pursed his lips. "Yes, you'd think they would have, don't you?" He placed his hands behind his head and was staring at Darian now from beneath hooded eyelids. "But since they didn't we must assume they felt this was not a truth that deserved to be told. In fact I doubt very much if you will find even a single scrap of paper that indicates you were adopted. Or a genuine birth certificate for that matter. Almost as if you don't exist."

"Rubbish. I'm quite sure my birth certificate is perfectly in order."

Edwards grinned. "Your father was a chief inspector of Scotland Yard. Don't you think he could manage a few forged documents?"

"But why? Why would he want to hide the fact I was adopted?"

"Isn't it obvious? The men who attacked the Pringles wanted to do a complete job. They wouldn't have liked it if one of their victims got away. You're supposed to be dead, Watley. And the fact that you're not had to be hidden very carefully, to avoid extremely nasty and gruesome consequences."

"So you're telling me..." He plunked down on the chair, flabbergasted and not doing a very good job hiding it. "You're telling me that I'm supposed to be officially dead?"

"The boy Tanner was declared dead, along with the rest of the family. A protective measure. And Broderick decided to adopt you himself, though you can't really call it an adoption as not a single document was ever signed. According to my information he simply made it look as if you were his."

Darian shook his head, completely bowled over. A man doesn't often discover he's not who he always thought he was, nor does he get the news from a well-known gangster.

"If you knew about this, Edwards, why didn't you try to use this information against me?" he asked now. "Or sell it to the highest bidder?"

Master Edwards shrugged. "Whatever you may think of me, I'm not a child killer, Watley. Nor do I condone the foul breed. I think what those men did was despicable. Murdering an entire family? I may be guilty of a lot of things but I never stooped that low. When I was offered this information I paid good money to acquire it, with the intention of keeping it off the street."

He stared at the man. "You bought this information to... protect me?"

Edwards played with a small puppet of a man being hanged. "Sometimes one does things that defy explanation, Watley. Make of it what you like."

It was hard to believe that the hardened gangster was truthful, Darian thought. It seemed so unlike Edwards to do something good for a change, and more specifically to help out a police officer. But he seemed truthful. "If that's the case, I owe you a debt of gratitude," he said simply.

Edwards looked him in the eye. "Yes, you do, Watley. And if the time comes, I might ask a little favor of you. Nothing much, mind you. Just something to return the kindness I showed you by not revealing your past."

And Master Edwards was back. "Of course you will," he said dryly, rising to his feet. "Why hadn't I seen that coming?"

"Oh, and one more thing. When you figure out who committed these horrible murders, please let me know. I may not look it, but I'm a sucker for a good murder mystery, and the Brunskill Manor Massacre has intrigued me for a very long time."

"Because you didn't carry it out, you mean?" he asked with arched brow.

"Like I said. I'm not a child killer, Watley. I just want to know who those monsters were."

"Wouldn't we all?" he asked, then was reminded of something. "Who sold you the information?"

Edwards grinned. "Now wouldn't you like to know?!"

Chapter 27

It only took Jarrett half a minute to reach the ground floor. And he'd just exited the building when a familiar face hove into view: Thorley Flax, suspiciously looking over his shoulder as if half expecting to be chased by a pack of ghosts. A sportsman like him, he'd probably taken the stairs.

"I've got something to tell you," he said when he caught up with Jarrett, "and I couldn't very well do it inside the apartment, could I?"

"Because they're listening to every word you say?" asked Jarrett excitedly. Finally here was a genuine clue, he thought. Something that was going to blow this entire case wide open, as the professionals would say.

"It's that old couple," lamented Thorley now. "They keep busting my chops. Whatever I do, they've got some nasty comment to make."

"That would be Etzel and Adele Cromwell?"

"That's right. The minute I moved in they started yapping and nagging. Said either I respected their presence and the fact that they were there first, or they would make my life a living hell. Since I liked the place I decided to play nice." He sighed. "It hasn't been easy, Jarrett."

"What do you mean?" he asked, curious. "What do they do?"

"Well, they don't like my music, for one thing, and they don't like the fact that I work out—heck, they don't like what I do for a living, period, and don't mind telling me loud and clear. Oh, and don't get them started on my diet. Especially Adele likes to point out I should eat meat and potatoes and not that 'vegetarian crap' I like to eat." He rolled his eyes.

"You're a vegetarian?" he asked, letting this eye wander over the man's impressive physique.

"Through and through. I hate it when people kill poor, innocent animals to feed themselves, Jarrett! It's criminal and should be punishable by law."

"Yes. Yes, I see what you mean," Jarrett said, blinking a little. He'd never met a vegetarian who looked as impressively muscular as this man mountain, he meant to say, and then he did say it, and Thorley grinned.

"Thanks, I guess. It's harder without taking in any animal proteins, of course, but it's possible, and I for one would advise you to treat the animal kingdom with the respect they're due, Jarrett. Treat animals the way you want to be treated yourself. So don't eat them unless you like to be eaten yourself, if you see what I mean."

"I will definitely give it some thought," he said, then remembered they hadn't stepped out of Brunskill Manor to talk about animal rights but about ghosts, so he decided to steer the conversation back on the right track. "So you're telling me that old couple is giving you a hard time, eh?"

"Busting my chops is an accurate description," he lamented. "They're always on my case, Jarrett, and if it weren't for the fact that this apartment is super convenient I'd have left a long time ago. And then there are the perks, of course, of living with a bunch of ghosts."

"What perks?" he asked curiously.

"Well, they guard the place with their lives, if you catch my drift. Or perhaps not their lives, exactly, as they're already dead, of course, but they do provide a decent sense of security. Some loser broke into the apartment only last week, and they scared him so much he must be halfway to China by now. And then it's also nice to have someone around, you know? I mean, I'm between girlfriends at the moment, and it gets lonely after a while."

"Yes, I can imagine," said Jarrett, a little disappointed.

His face fell. "They also told me how they died. Nasty business."

Now this was interesting, so Jarrett pricked up his ears. "Did they tell you who did it? Who killed them and their family?"

"Well, no, actually. The killers wore masks, so they assumed they were robbers, looking for valuables. Brunskill Manor was one of the architectural jewels of the neighborhood, back in the day, and those prowlers must have thought its owners were pretty loaded. That they had jewelry lying around and heaps of cash. While in fact they were poor as church mice, of course."

"Poor as church mice but living in a place like this? I find that hard to believe."

Thorley shrugged. "There was a rumor about a stash of gold being hidden somewhere inside the walls, but apparently that's all it was: a rumor."

"No way!"

"Yes, way!"

"Well, you have your ghosts, I have mine," said Jarrett. "I've spent some time at Emmanuella Sheetenhelm's place, and her apartment is inhabited by no less than two ghosts. Maybe even three. I had a long chat with Leandra Pringle last night and she told me the whole story about the horrible massacre of that night, and that the men who killed her are coming..."

He bit his tongue, not wanting to cause alarm.

"Go on," Thorley prompted eagerly. "She told you the killers are..."

"She said the killers are coming back to finish the job," he said reluctantly.

Thorley's eyes went wide. "Finish what job? You don't mean..."

Jarrett nodded. "Kill the ones they didn't get the first time around."

"I don't get it," said the bodybuilding Chippendale. "Who else is left? They're all dead, right? Except for Cicily Pringle, but she doesn't live here anymore, and Callesta Cromwell, and Adele told me she moved to Australia."

"I think she meant you and the other present occupants of the house," said Jarrett carefully. "There's something they want at Brunskill Manor, and they're coming to get it this time, and remove anyone who gets in their way."

Thorley stared at him with a worried frown. "That's not good, Jarrett."

"No," he agreed, "getting murdered isn't my idea of a fun evening either."

"So what do you suggest?" Thorley asked, licking his lips.

"That you join Bruna Mars and her daughter and the Horrockses and move into my suite at the Ritz Carlton for the time being. At least until this whole thing blows over."

"Stay at your place until..."

"Until we manage to solve the case and rid Brunskill Manor of its ghosts."

Thorley rubbed his chin thoughtfully. "I don't know, Jarrett. I must confess the old couple has grown on me. Nowadays they even let me play my music loud, and I think I saw Etzel headbang to Metallica yesterday."

"So you'd rather they stick around?" he asked, incredulous.

The big guy thought about this for a moment, then finally confessed, "Yeah. At first it was pretty annoying, but we kinda became friends, and these days they're almost tolerable. Though I have to keep reminding Adele to stay away from the bathroom when I take a shower. Even though Etzel never fails to scold her for it, she likes to drop in when I'm in the shower."

"Yes, I can see how that might be annoying," said Jarrett, trying to suppress the images these words conjured up. Personally he could sympathize with the little old lady. If a hunkishly handsome male like Thorley Flax lived in his apartment, and he was capable of drifting through walls, he'd have a hard time staying away from the bathroom himself. He quickly suppressed the enticing visuals, however, and said, "At least we have to solve the mystery of what happened that night, and then the ghosts will be able to choose whether they still want to stick around after that, or move on."

"Yeah, that sounds reasonable," said Thorley. "But I, for one, don't feel like running away, Jarrett. If those guys are coming back, I want to be here to make them pay for what they did to Etzel and Adele and their family. Besides, they must be old guys by now, right?"

"A good deal older than they were the last time," he agreed. Though math had never been his strong suit, he figured that if thirty-five years had passed since the Brunskill Manor Massacre, those years would probably have to be added to the perpetrators' ages, which would make them a good deal older than they'd been the first time around.

"So when are they coming? I want to be prepared."

"Well, the consensus seems to be pretty soon. And Leandra

indicated her missing son will be there to take revenge as well. So the place might just turn into some kind of battlefield. Are you quite sure you want to stick around?"

"Sure I'm sure," said Thorley, landing a balled fist into the palm of his hand. A determined gleam had come into his eye. "I'm going to make them pay for what they did. And I'm sure Etzel and Adele feel the same way. Let them come. The welcoming committee will be ready and waiting."

Oh, dear, thought Jarrett. This wasn't good. He abhorred violence, and he was already regretting having gotten involved in this mess in the first place. Dealing with ghosts and helping them solve their murders was one thing, but facing vicious killers who had murdered an entire family was quite another.

Chapter 28

When Harry returned to the flat, she was surprised to find that a meeting was in progress, its participants trying to drown each other out by screaming at the tops of their lungs while a very large man with bulging muscles sat on the sofa staring in front of him with a vacuous expression on his face.

"Um, guys?" she asked, after stepping into the fray. "What's going on?"

Jarrett and Darian, the participants in question, both looked up when she strode into their midst, Buckley in tow.

"Christ, Harry!" Darian yelled. "This is not the time to play games!"

"Play games?" she asked with a frown. "What do you mean?"

"That!" cried Darian, pointing at Buckley. "You know very well Buckley is dead and gone, so why carry around a 3D image of him? It's not funny!"

She eyed the policeman sharply. "For your information, Darian, Buckley isn't dead and gone. He's very much..." She was going to say 'alive and kicking' but that would have been a lie, obviously, so instead she said, "He's very much here with us. This is, in fact, his ghost."

Buckley now waved at Darian, who blanched considerably. "Hello, there, Inspector Watley. How are you doing on this fine day? I never got the opportunity to thank you for conducting an excellent investigation into my murder. Much obliged, sir. Well done. Taxpayers' money well spent and all."

Darian produced an audible gasp, staggered back, then plunked down on the couch right next to the very big, burly man, who gave him a gentle pat on the back. "I know just how you feel, little buddy," he said consolingly.

"I don't think I'll ever get used to this," Darian muttered feebly.

"You will," said the bodybuilder. "In due course you'll learn to love the breed."

"Hey, Buckley," said Jarrett, less shocked. "I thought you'd moved on?"

"Well, I thought so too, Jarrett. But as it happens the powers that be granted me a special hall pass so I can set up Harry's security detail. Make absolutely certain she turns the Wraith Wranglers into a resounding success."

"Buckley's going to be the third partner in our Wraith Wranglers business, Jarrett," Harry explained.

"Wonderful," murmured Jarrett, directing a kindling eye at Darian, indicating he had some unfinished business with the Scotland Yardie.

"What's going on with you two?" Harry now asked. "And who is your new friend?" she added, directing a curious glance at the newcomer.

"Oh, this is Thorley," said Jarrett. "Thorley Flax, meet Harry McCabre. Harry, meet Thorley. He lives in the Etzel and Adele Cromwell apartment."

"They're my roomies," said the big guy with a grin. "Spooky

roomies."

"He's volunteering to help us thwart the dangers that are encroaching."

While these introductions were made, it didn't escape Harry's attention that Darian had sunk into a moody silence, and was staring before him with a faraway look on his handsome face. She wondered what was going on.

"Are you quite all right, Darian?" she asked, approaching the copper.

"Mh?" asked Darian vaguely. "What's that?"

"What's going on?" she asked with a frown. "You look... on edge."

"I'll tell you what's going on," said Jarrett. "The man's a Pringle! Can you believe it? He's the long-lost son of Leandra and Anselm Pringle. None other than Tanner Pringle himself! Master Edwards told him the news and we're all quite shocked."

"Not least of all me," muttered Darian.

Harry's jaw dropped. "You're Tanner Pringle?"

Darian eyed her somberly. "Looks like. At least that's what that old crook Master Edwards told me. Talk about a bombshell revelation."

"But..." Harry stared from Darian to Jarrett. "How is that possible?!"

"The only ones who can answer that are my parents, obviously," said Darian. "Which is why I've called this emergency meeting. Only they haven't shown up yet." He glanced at his watch. "I wonder what's keeping them."

Harry suddenly felt her legs go weak and she plunked down on a chair. Darian Watley was Tanner Pringle? "But how? Why? When?"

Darian lifted his shoulders and continued to stare before

him, looking shell-shocked. "Beats me, Harry. All I know is what Edwards told me. Which wasn't much, I can tell you."

"It was quite enough," commented Jarrett.

Just then, the doorbell rang. "That will be Dad," Darian said.

"I'll go," said Jarrett. "This whole thing has got me so rattled I can't seem to sit still for even a second."

Harry now joined Darian on the couch and placed a hand on his arm. He looked up, his face a mask of worry. "Are you all right?" she asked solicitously. "The news must have come as quite a shock to you."

"Oh, yes, it has. But in the interests of self-preservation I've more or less decided to refuse to accept the big revelation until I get confirmation."

He looked up when Broderick strode in, grumbling, "What's all this nonsense about an emergency meeting? I've got better things to do than to keep showing up in your mother's apartment, Darian, don't you know?"

Darian cleared his throat, looking pained. "Dad, I've received some very upsetting news, and I wanted to run it by you first, before Mother arrives."

Broderick took off his hat and scarf and draped them over a chair. "Yes, what is it?" he asked impatiently. "Out with it, boy. Out with it!" he cried.

His eyes were nervously flitting about, as if fully expecting to see more ghosts popping out of the woodwork. When his eyes briefly flickered over Buckley and then away again, it was obvious he didn't think the man was a ghost at all, but simply part of the group. Well, apart from the big gash on the back of his head, he looked fine.

Darian directed a serious look at his father. "Dad, is it true that..." He swallowed, then tried again. "Is it true that I'm...

Tanner Pringle?"

Broderick started violently. "Eh, what? I mean to say, what, what?"

"I just had a long talk with Bill Edwards. You remember Edwards?"

"The East End crime king," acknowledged Broderick, his eyes shifty now, as if he had something to hide, which apparently he had.

"He told me that my real name is Tanner Pringle and that you and Mother took me in when you discovered me alive in this house, figuring it was safer for me to become part of your family than put me up for adoption."

Broderick's eyes had narrowed considerably, but it was a testament to his policeman's training that he didn't freak out or make a spectacle of himself.

Then, finally, he nodded once. "It's true, son. You are indeed Tanner Pringle, and your mother and I did adopt you and raised you as our own."

Darian's eyes closed and he emitted a little grunt of surprise. Then his eyes shot open again. "So you're not my father and Em is not my mother."

"I'm your father in every way that counts, son," said Broderick emphatically, "except perhaps that you're not my flesh and blood."

"A minor detail," murmured Jarrett.

"But why?" cried Darian now. "And why didn't you tell me?"

Chapter 29

Broderick, who now stood wide-legged before the gathering, hands firmly clasped behind his back, gave Darian an intensely serious look. "We didn't want to endanger you, Darian. When I found you, you were stuffed beneath a cupboard in the living room." He pointed to a corner of the room. "Right there. Leandra must have shoved you beneath it when the men showed up and began their murderous rampage. She'd also stuck a bib in your mouth to keep you quiet and when I discovered you, you were barely breathing." He shook his head. "I don't know why I concealed you inside my raincoat and took you home. Instinct, I guess. It was obvious someone had wanted to murder the entire family, and the fact that you were only a baby wouldn't have stopped them. I figured the only way to keep you safe was to spirit you away from the scene, and let whoever was responsible for this monstrous massacre think you hadn't survived."

"I don't get it," said Darian now softly. "Why didn't you hand me over to one of my two surviving aunts? Callesta Cromwell or Cicily Pringle?"

"Cicily was only a child herself, and Callesta…" Broderick hesitated. "I had reason to believe she was behind the massacre herself. There was bad blood between her and your mother, and even though nothing was ever proven, I never felt sanguine handing you over to her, or even letting on you'd survived."

"But why you... Dad? Why not leave me on the doorstep of some orphanage? Nobody would ever have known."

Broderick's eyes softened. "That was my initial idea as well. I took you home with me that night wanting to think things through, but when Em saw you... she fell in love. There's no other word for it. We..." He swallowed away a lump in his throat. "We'd been wanting to have a baby for the longest time, but there was a problem with, um, with my swimmers and with Em's, um, pool. Apparently my swimmers weren't strong enough," he quickly went on, looking distinctly uncomfortable now, "and your mother's pool proved a hostile environment, so... in any case, when I brought you home that Christmas Eve, your mother felt you were a gift from God, and when I told her the circumstances in which I found you she simply decided to keep you."

"Just like that?" Darian asked softly.

"Just like that. I took care of some paperwork and you went from being Tanner Pringle to being Darian Watley."

"In one night."

Broderick nodded. "That's right." He eyed his son a little uncertainly. "I can understand your shock, Darian, or even your anger. I know we should have told you the truth, but we decided not to. Make sure nobody knew our secret, not even you. We did it to protect you, you see that, right?" When Darian didn't respond, he added, "As Darian Watley, son of a chief inspector, you were safe from these men. They're still out there, son. They might still be targeting you for all we know."

"Somehow the story leaked, Dad."

"I can't imagine how," said Broderick with a frown.

"Master Edwards knew. I don't know how he knew, but he knew."

"I never told anyone, and neither did Em," Broderick grumbled, fingering his bristling white mustache.

"You must have discussed it with someone," said Harry now. "Or else how did you get him the right paperwork?"

"Oh, that was easy enough," said Broderick. "I simply pulled some strings. I arranged everything directly with the mayor's assistant. She…" He paused, his brow puckering into a frown. "You don't think she told Edwards, do you?" he asked, as if addressing the question to himself.

"Who is she?" asked Darian now.

Broderick stared at him, then said, almost absentmindedly, "I never told her you were Tanner Pringle. I never told anyone. But I was the lead investigator, and the story of Tanner Pringle was headline news at the time."

"And then you suddenly showed up with a baby," said Darian, nodding.

"Perhaps there were people who knew about your… swimmers?" asked Jarrett with a slight grin. "To them it must have seemed strange that suddenly, and on the same day the Pringle kid disappeared no less, you acquired a baby boy."

Broderick gave him a dark look. "Our medical issues were nobody's business."

"Still, people talk, Broderick," Harry said. "You know that."

He nodded. "Perhaps you're right. The mayor's assistant might have put two and two together, and figured out you were Tanner Pringle. Still, I find it highly unlikely."

"Who was this woman, Dad?" asked Darian again.

"Isla Reed," said Broderick. "And she couldn't have told Master Edwards. She died a couple of years ago. But her husband could have," he added thoughtfully. "Gary Reed was always an inveterate drunk and a gambler. He would have sold his own mother for a drink."

"A gambler? Like Anselm Pringle?" asked Darian.

Broderick nodded. "If Isla ever had any suspicions, she might have told Gary." Broderick stared at this son. "This means your life's in danger, Darian. Who knows how many others know about you. If indeed Gary Reed is the source, he might even have sold the information to your family's killers."

Broderick and Darian stared at each other, then Darian smiled. "You're still my dad, Dad," he said quietly. "No matter who my real parents were."

Broderick displayed a crooked smile. "Thank you, son," he said hoarsely, and both men shared a well-meant hug that brought tears to Harry's eyes.

Whatever this tragedy had spawned, at least something good had come of it. Darian had discovered a secret from his past, and instead of creating a rift between him and Broderick, it had brought both men closer together.

And as she thought this, the door swung open and Em strode in, her long blond hair all shiny and perfectly coiffed, and when she saw the group gathered in her apartment, she cried, "I leave this place for two minutes and some new tragedy takes place? What happened?" she asked when both Darian and Broderick looked at her with serious expressions on their faces.

"He knows, Em," said Broderick.

"He knows what?" she demanded, dropping two bulky bags to the floor.

Broderick nodded, and simply repeated, "He knows."

Em let out a loud cry, and brought her hands to her face. "Why?!" she cried. "Why did you tell him?! I thought we agreed never to—"

"I didn't tell him. He heard it from some sleazy crime lord."

Em directed a look of anguish at her son. "Oh, Darian," she

said feebly, staggering forward on high heels. "Darian, darling."

"It's all right, Mother," he said, and caught her deftly in his arms. And then, for the first time since Harry made her acquaintance, Em was crying.

"This stuff is more entertaining than the Kardashians," a voice muttered next to Harry, and she saw it was Thorley Flax, who sat watching the scene as if it was playing out on the big screen. And she had to agree with the guy. As far as entertainment value went, this definitely topped the Kardashians.

Chapter 30

"I think we need to talk to some people," said Harry.

"Which people?" asked Jarrett, who was still following the denouement of the Darian Watley/Tanner Pringle affair with rapt attention.

"Cicily Pringle, for instance," she said, "and Callesta Cromwell."

"Can't be done," grunted Broderick. "Callesta lives in Australia these days. Emigrated right after the tragedy and hasn't been back since."

"We could Skype," Harry suggested.

Broderick stared at her, as if he'd never heard of this nifty new way of communicating before.

"Or FaceTime. Or simply call her on the phone," she explained.

"Great idea, Harry," said Buckley. "And if all else fails, I can always pop over there and interview her in person."

"Let's... try to interview her the old-fashioned way, shall we?" she suggested. She could only imagine how Callesta would react if suddenly a ghost appeared on her doorstep, or, rather, popped out of her kitchen wall.

"If we're going to do this, we better do it right," said Darian, still the policeman of the small band of friends and associates. "We should talk to Gary Reed as well. See what he knows and who he told about my secret."

"What about the rest of the ghosts?" asked Thorley now. And when the others all turned to him, he shrugged. "There must be a ton of ghosts we haven't spoken to. Brothers, sisters, uncles, aunts... Those Pringles and Cromwells were quite the breeders," he added with a grin.

"Yes, so far we've only heard from Abigail," said Jarrett. "Perhaps it's time we talked to..." And here he showed what a promising detective he really was, for he consulted a little leather-bound notebook. "Tawnya, Finley and Darren." He snapped the notebook shut. "As Thorley suggested, we need to talk to the entire brood."

Harry saw that Em and Broderick had naturally flocked together at the news that their son had found out he wasn't really their son after all. They now stood huddled together, talking in hushed tones. She thought they looked cute, and Darian seemed to think so too, for he eyed them with affection. Perhaps this entire incident would bring the former couple closer together, and Em would finally accept Broderick hadn't touched that woman.

"So how are we doing this, you guys?" she now asked.

"I'll see what I can find out from Gary Reed," Darian said, his face turning serious once more. "I'll make that guy sing like a canary."

"No, I'll make him sing like a canary," interrupted his father. "If anyone should talk to the guy, it's me, son," he explained with a determined look on his face. "After all, if I hadn't gone to Isla Reed, your secret would be safe."

"Then I'll go with you, Dad," said Darian. "Let's do this together."

"And I'll talk to Cicily, shall I?" Harry suggested.

"Count me in as well," said Jarrett.

"So who's going to call Callesta Cromwell?" asked Buckley.

"I'll have a pop at her, shall I?" asked Thorley with a grin. "I want to know what's going on in this house as much as you guys do," he explained.

And so it was settled. Harry and Jarrett would talk to Cicily Pringle, Thorley would try to get in touch with Callesta Cromwell, and Darian and his dad would go round to Gary Reed's place and see what they could find out from that man.

"What about me?" asked Em. "What do you want me to do?"

Buckley eyed her keenly. "If you don't mind, the two of us could try to get in touch with the members of the Pringle family we haven't met yet."

"We'll do our interviews and meet back here, all right?" suggested Harry.

"Great," grunted Darian. "Hopefully we'll get some answers." He clapped his hands. "All right, people, let's do this. Let's roll. And let's be careful out there."

For some reason, he reminded Harry of some old cop show, though for the life of her she couldn't remember which one. Only that it had something to do with a hill, a street and the blues.

Chapter 31

"Do you really think she'll talk?" Harry asked. Jarrett was steering his yellow Maserati through morning traffic. It was actually the first time Harry had ever seen him drive a car himself. Usually he moved around in his big black Rolls Royce, chauffeured by Deshawn. But since the valet was now playing host to the Horrockses and the Marses, he had to make do with the Maserati, one of the more modest specimens in his extensive collection.

"Oh, I'm sure she will," said Jarrett with his customary confidence.

Harry soon found her thoughts drifting back to the Tanner Pringle bombshell. "I wonder why this Gary Reed—if it's him who spilled the beans—only talked now," she said as she stared out at the buildings that zoomed past. The sidewalks were filled with people late for work and shoppers eager to get to their favorite stores. She'd rolled down the window and a breeze ruffled her blond bob. In spite of traffic, the air smelled fresh and sweet.

"It's one of the mysteries we have to solve," said Jarrett, as he honked his horn at a pedestrian who seemed to feel the street belonged to him.

"In two hundred yards, turn right," the metallic voice of the GPS intoned.

Soon they were parked in front of a modest high-rise, and Harry looked up at the tall building and all of its ten floors. She frowned when she saw a small sign indicating this building housed Zephyr Securities & Loans.

"Are you sure this is where we'll find Cicily Pringle?" she asked, figuring perhaps Jarrett needed to run an errand first.

"Sure I'm sure," said Jarrett, then placed a hand on her arm when she started to exit the car. "Um, Harry? There's something I haven't told you."

"What is it?" she asked, though she had some idea what was coming.

"The reason I wanted this assignment is because..."

"Cicily works for you," she said.

He nodded. "Yep. Has worked for us for some time, actually."

"That's great," she said. "If she knows you she'll be more inclined to talk."

"Um, actually, no," he said, casting down his eyes.

"What do you mean? If she works for you, you're her boss, right?"

He sighed. "When I was a young whippersnapper, Dad had the bright idea that I should learn about the business from one of the number crunchers."

"Cicily."

"Right. So he had me intern as her assistant for a couple of months." He winced. "Let's just say I didn't make the greatest impression."

"She's one of your father's accountants?" she asked, seeing the picture.

"These days she's the Zephyr Group's CFO, actually."

"Ouch. Well, I'm sure she'll talk to you, Jarrett. You're still her employer's son, right? How bad can it be?"

How bad it was soon became clear, when, upon being led into Cicily Pringle's office, her face displayed her marked displeasure at being reacquainted with one who at one time had been her trusty assistant.

"Jarrett," she snapped, without offering him a hand.

"Cicily," he muttered. "This is a good friend of mine, Harry McCabre."

"Yes." The woman studied Harry carefully. "The ghost hunter," she said, her voice indicating she was not a great supporter of this new venture in Jarrett's life.

"That's me," said Harry, as chipper as she managed under the icy glare of the other woman. In her mind Cicily Pringle had been a college student, and seeing her now came as something of a shock. Of course, thirty-five years had passed since the tragedy, and Cicily was now closer to Emmanuella's age. She was a dark-haired, distinguished woman, her head held high, her lips thin and disapproving, and her eyes an icy gray. She was dressed in a gray power suit, and looked positively forbidding, Harry thought.

The office itself was one of those sterile places, where nothing reminded the visitor that here worked an actual human being and not a robot.

From the window, she could see the London Eye, below it the glittering vista of the River Thames snaking past it.

"The reason for this visit," said Harry, when Jarrett failed to kickstart the interview, "is that some residents of the house formerly known as Brunskill Manor, have asked us to look into the history of that particular building."

Cicily's eyes went a little colder still, and she promptly rose to her feet.

"Miss McCabre, let me save you the trouble. This interview is at an end," she announced. "Brunskill Manor and the events connected with it are not topics I care to discuss at this point. Thank you for coming, and goodbye."

Chapter 32

Harry stared at the CFO, and her outstretched hand. Then she decided to steel herself. She hadn't come all this way to be thrown out now. "The thing is," she began, "that a very dear friend of mine now occupies one of the apartments at your former residence, and… certain events have led her to believe that her life may be in danger."

The woman frowned. "In danger, how?" Then a cold smile curved her lips. "Oh, I see what you mean. Ghosts, right? Isn't that what you are into these days, Jarrett? The hunt for ghosts and the exploitation of the gullible?"

"This has nothing to do with ghosts," Jarrett said, stubbornly remaining seated. "This has to do with certain threats that have been made against our mutual friend, Emmanuella Sheetenhelm, and some of the other occupants."

"Threats? What threats?"

"Death threats," said Harry, taking a leaf out of Jarrett's book.

"Oh," said the woman, then slowly sat down again. "And what does this have to do with me?"

"These… threats seem to be coming from the same people who were responsible for the Brunskill Manor tragedy of 1981," said Harry.

"How do you know?" she asked without missing a beat. "The killers were never identified."

"Oh, we have our reasons," said Jarrett airily.

"I'll bet you have," she said icily. "My suggestion? Have your friend and the other occupants contact Scotland Yard. They'll know what to do." She rose again. "Now if there's nothing more, I have work to do. Real work," she added as an aside to Jarrett. "And if you think I won't mention this latest escapade of yours to your father you're mistaken, Jarrett."

"Please do," said Jarrett, smoothing a crease in his trousers.

She stood for a moment, seemingly unsure what to do, then said, "I said all I had to say about the tragedy that befell my family years ago. To the police *and* the press. And I would appreciate it if you'd leave well enough alone. This is not one of your 'fun' pet projects, Jarrett. You're dealing with people's lives now. Real people and real tragedies."

"It is just such a tragedy we're trying to stop," said Harry. "My friend Em... she's in real danger. I can't tell you how we know, but this is not a joke, Mrs. Pringle."

"Langton," she said automatically. "I go by my husband's name now."

"Please, Mrs. Langton," said Harry passionately. "This won't take more than a few minutes of your time. Your assistance might save a lot of lives."

Cicily Langton stood regally for a moment, then she nodded. "Five minutes," she said curtly. "And then I really have to ask you to leave."

"I'm sorry for springing this on you," said Jarrett. "I understand it's not much fun having to be reminded of what happened over and over again."

"Not much fun?" she snapped. "I see you're still the same

insensitive callous youth you always were, Jarrett. Last time you unleashed a nest of white mice into my office…"

Harry stared at Jarrett, who muttered, "Don't ask."

"… and if that wasn't enough you set off a stink bomb in the middle of a very important meeting with a delegation from one of China's top telecommunications companies. It's a miracle we didn't lose the contract."

"I'm sorry," murmured Jarrett with bowed head, though he didn't seem to be very sorry, Harry thought. In fact she had the distinct impression he was having trouble suppressing his laughter, the recollection of his youthful transgressions apparently a great source of amusement.

"Is there anything you can tell us about the killers, Mrs. Langton?" asked Harry softly, deciding to take over the interview. "Any clue as to their identity?"

The CFO shook her head. "I went through all of this years ago, with that policeman…" She frowned. "What was his name again? Watford, Watney?"

"Broderick Watley," Harry said. "Emmanuella Sheetenhelm is his wife, actually. She moved in a couple of months ago, along with her son, who's also a police officer."

She studied Harry for a moment. "Yes, that's right," she said. "Broderick Watley. It's quite a coincidence, isn't it, that his wife and son would be living at Brunskill Manor now. And she's been getting death threats?"

Harry nodded. She could see how the story didn't make much sense without revealing that it were, indeed, ghosts who'd led them to this point. But she had the impression mentioning this fact wouldn't get them anywhere.

"I don't know what to tell you, Miss McCabre. You spoke to Chief Inspector Watley. He knows what happened that night. I wasn't home, and wasn't even allowed inside when it was over. I never set foot in that house again and I never will," she said with a slight tremor in her voice.

"You had a boyfriend?" Harry asked. "Do you still keep in touch?"

She blinked. "No, we don't. I haven't seen him in thirty-five years." She got up again, and this time there would be no reprieve, Harry saw, so she also rose to her feet, and so did Jarrett. And as Cicily ushered them out of her office, she told Jarrett, "Why don't you do your father and us a big favor and drop this ghost hunting nonsense, Jarrett? Once your father retires, this company needs a responsible adult at the helm, not a child of thirty-one."

And with these words, she closed the door behind them, and Jarrett breathed a sigh of relief. "That went pretty well, don't you think?"

Chapter 33

According to Broderick's file, Cicily's ex-boyfriend's name was Alistair Adair, and he ran a dingy auto repair shop a stone's throw from King's Cross. As they walked into the shop, Harry thought that if ever she owned a car, she wouldn't want to be seen dead in here. It looked like the place where old cars came to die, judging from a number of wrecks littering the filthy shop.

A man in greasy overalls came ambling up to them, rubbing his greasy hands on a rag, a cap covering his equally greasy head and a cigarette dangling from his lips. She took one look at the floor, covered in oil and gasoline, and thought that here strode a man who liked to live dangerously. Some form of hipster fungoid growth covered his face, and when he spoke, the thing seemed to move.

"What's up, guv'nor?!" he yelled. "Maserati in need of a tune-up?"

"No, the car's fine," said Jarrett, holding his hands behind his back in case the mechanic made an attempt to grab them. "We would like a word with Alistair Adair, if that's possible."

"That's me," said the guy, lifting his cap to show thinning red hair. He was the same age as Cicily, Harry guessed, but looked a lot seedier than the prim and proper CFO. In fact they looked like they came from different worlds. Still, at one point in the past, their paths had briefly crossed.

"We're looking into the death of the Pringle family," Jarrett continued.

Alistair frowned. "Pringle? You mean that massacre back in the eighties?"

"That's the one."

"But that's ages ago!" he cried, incredulous. "What are you, coppers?"

"We're not, actually," said Harry. "We've been asked by the people who live in the building formerly known as Brunskill Manor to look into the matter." She didn't feel like giving this man a lot of information.

He scratched his head. "Yes, well, I don't have any. Information, I mean."

"You and Cicily Pringle used to be an item back in the day?" asked Jarrett.

He grinned widely, displaying two rows of crooked, yellowed teeth. "We sure were, mate. She was sweet on me, that one. That's why she gave me that money in the first place." He frowned. "You know about that, right?"

"Of course," lied Jarrett. "She gave you money to..."

"Start this garage, of course," said Alistair.

"Of course."

"And when was this, exactly?" asked Harry.

Alistair thought for a moment, then grinned again. "Come on. I'll show you." And as he led the way to a shed built against the side of the shop, he called out, "I was never any good with dates. Or numbers, for that matter!"

He opened the door and stepped inside. Reluctantly, Harry and Jarrett followed him in and watched him kneel down in a corner and open a small safe with a deft flick of the wrist. He took out an old and tattered ledger and slapped it down on his metal desk, shoving a bunch of paperwork out of the way. This place was an accountant's nightmare, Harry thought.

"Look here. This is the original document, see?"

Harry watched as he produced a piece of paper, apparently written in a child's scrawl. It said that Cicily Pringle donated Alistair Adair the sum of five thousand pounds. He stabbed at a date on the document. It read January 15, 1982. Both Harry and Jarrett stared at it. This was only a few weeks after the massacre. Probably paid from Cicily's inheritance, Harry thought.

"It was very nice of Cicily to give you the money," she said.

"Well, this was our dream, see? We were going to do this together. I knew something about car mechanics and Cicily was going to try and raise the money. We were even gonna get married. Only her brother wasn't having any of it. Said I wasn't good enough for his little sister. She promised she wasn't going to listen to him, that we were like Romeo and the other one, um..."

"Juliet?" suggested Jarrett.

"That's the one! Kept telling me our love was forever, but then those murders happened..." He shrugged. "The trauma of that particular drama drove us apart, didn't it? As a drama of such magnitude invariably does."

He sounded as if he'd been watching too many Lifetime movies, Harry thought. "If you weren't an item anymore, why did she give you the money?"

He smiled. "That's Cicily Pringle for you. A promise is a promise. Told me it was her farewell gift. A sign of a love that should have lasted years."

"Right," said Jarrett dubiously.

As Alistair talked, Harry cast a look around. And then suddenly something caught her eye and the blood froze in her veins. Alistair must have caught her surprise, for he eyed her suspiciously, then said, "If there's nothing more... All this talk of the past has greatly upset me, I don't mind saying."

Jarrett raised an eyebrow in surprise, and the other one when Harry gave him a prod in the ribs, indicating it was time to go. "Well," he said, thrusting out his hand, then instantly retracting it, "thanks for your time, Alistair."

Once they were outside, he asked, "What was that all about?!"

Harry waited until they were in the car, and the doors were closed, then said slowly, "There was a picture frame depicting Alistair Adair and Cicily Pringle. Must have been taken in 1981, judging from their youthful looks."

"And?"

"There was a third person in that picture."

He gave her a sideways look of surprise as she watched in the rearview mirror how Alistair slowly disappeared from view, still staring after them.

"Who?"

She paused, then said, "Thorley Flax. Looking exactly like he does now."

Jarrett's eyes widened in shock. "You mean..."

She nodded. "Thorley Flax is a ghost."

Chapter 34

*D*arian pressed his finger on the bell a third time, this time keeping it there as he heard the sound of the bell resonate inside.

"It's no use, Darian," said his father. "Either he's home and too drunk to open the door, or he's out." He stared around himself, then focused his attention on a small pub on the corner of the street. "Let's pop over there and see if they've seen our man," he suggested.

"Good idea," he grunted, and both men trudged over. "I'm glad we talked things through, Dad," he said. "It can't have been easy for you and Mother to keep this under wraps all this time."

"No, it certainly wasn't," confirmed Broderick. "There were so many times I wanted to tell you, son, but your mother made me promise not to."

"Why? Did she think I was going to freak out or something?"

His father gave him a serious look. "She thought once you knew you'd go after your family's killers, and she didn't want you to endanger yourself."

"Well, looks like the killers are now coming after me," he riposted.

They entered the pub, and allowed their eyes to adjust to the relative darkness of the place. Even at this early hour they were open for business, and when Broderick nudged him and said, "There he is," he looked in the direction indicated and saw a man in his sixties, looking like hell.

His bloodshot eyes stared vacantly into space, his sallow skin sported a gray stubble and he was nursing a very large glass of lager. When they joined him at his table and introduced themselves, he had a hard time figuring out who they were, but then finally he seemed to recognize Broderick.

"You look like a politician," he said, slurring his words. "And I don't like politicians."

"Why?" asked Darian. "What did politicians ever do to you?"

"Took away my wife," said the man. "Politics killed her."

"You're Gary Reed, right?" asked Broderick. "Husband of Isla Reed?"

"That you killed," insisted the man.

"Why don't you explain that to me, Gary," said Darian.

He shrugged. "Not much to explain. Isla worked for the mayor's office, didn't she? For years and years and... well, for years. Then one day—poof! She was let go."

"And why was that?" asked Darian.

Gary swept his arm across the table, barely missing his pint of lager. "New regime swept in and old regime was swept out. They did an audit and discovered she was a bit too matey with some crook."

"What crook?" asked Broderick, to whom this all seemed news.

"Bill Edwards. They weren't exactly paying her the big bucks," he said, "so she had to make a bit of money on the side, if you know what I mean."

Darian raked his fingers through his mane. "I do see what you mean," he grunted. So that's how Edwards had found out about him. From Isla Reed.

"Fake documents, passports, whatnot," Gary muttered.

"How did she die, Gary?" asked Broderick now, his voice uncharacteristically soft.

Gary seemed surprised by this kindness, and tears sprang to his eyes. "Cancer took her, didn't it? But really it was the shame. She never got her life in order after losing that job. It was everything to her. It meant respect and the friendship of great colleagues. After she was sacked she was never the same again. And of course I didn't help." He heaved his pint. "In fact it's fair to say that between the mayor and my fondness for drink we pretty much shoved her in the grave. She simply let go, you know. My beautiful Isla went out like a light. So you see what I mean when I say that politics killed her?"

It was a testament to Master Edwards's oddly quirky sense of morals that he'd never revealed his secret, Darian thought. So he'd been right after all, that he didn't condone child killers, and had never sold the information to anyone. Even amongst crooks there was a certain code of honor, apparently.

"I think we're done here," said Broderick, after a commiserating glance at Gary Reed. Though the man probably didn't deserve their compassion, it was hard not to sympathize with his plight. And as they both rose and walked to the door, Darian saw he'd missed a call from Harry. And as he listened to her message, his eyes widened into a look of surprise.

"We have to get back to the house," he quickly told his father. Broderick looked up in alarm, surprised by the sharp edge to his son's voice.

"Why? What's the emergency?"

His eyes bored into his dad's, conveying the urgency of the message. "Thorley Flax. He's one of Alistair Adair's associates... and a ghost."

"Oh, Christ," grunted Broderick. "Em's there, and she's alone with him!"

Chapter 35

As she and Jarrett hurried back to the apartment, Harry thought about what all this meant: if Thorley Flax was a ghost, he must have died years ago, to still look so young and athletic. On the other hand, this could mean nothing, of course. Perhaps he simply didn't want anyone to know he'd died.

"This could be a false alarm," she now said. "Thorley might just be one of those shy and reticent ghosts who doesn't like people to know he's dead."

"I don't know," grumbled Jarrett, his eye fixed on the road. "He should have told us. Besides, he doesn't strike me as the shy retiring type. At all."

"No, he doesn't, does he?" she asked, chewing her lip. She tried Em's cell again, but just like the last five times it went straight to voicemail. In desperation she called out, "Buckley! Are you there? Tell us what's going on."

She thought it was strange that Buckley hadn't said anything about Thorley. Ghosts recognize ghosts, don't they? If so, why hadn't he noticed that Thorley was a ghost? Of course, they'd never indicated he wasn't. Perhaps Buckley thought they all knew that Thorley was actually dead.

"And to think I liked the guy so much," grumbled Jarrett. "I mean, that body, that washboard tummy, that cute smile..." He sighed. "Those dimples."

In spite of their predicament, Harry laughed at this.

"What's so funny?"

"What's not? A wraith wrangler falling in love with a wraith? It's hilarious, Jarrett."

"No, it isn't," he insisted, his hands gripping the wheel. "I've been the victim of deception. He tried to deceive me into falling for him. It's not nice."

"I don't think Deshawn would have been so easily fooled, though."

"No, Deshawn would have seen right through him," Jarrett confirmed.

"Literally," added Harry. "And now I wonder why we didn't."

"He simply doesn't look like a ghost. For one thing he doesn't have that... flimsy quality. The guy's quite solid. When he pressed me in his arms I could feel the strength and solidity of his body. And his sweat." He sighed again.

She gave her partner a sideways glance. "He pressed you into his arms?"

"He needed to get me out of the apartment and he wanted to make sure that Etzel and Adele wouldn't overhear him whispering something in my ear." Jarrett's eyes went wide. "Oh, my God! He didn't want me to talk to Grandma and Grandpa Cromwell! Of course! If I had, they would have told me Thorley was a ghost, just like them!"

"And perhaps their attacker."

Jarrett shook his head. "The man doesn't strike me as a killer, Harry. Like you said, perhaps he simply died and doesn't want anyone to know?"

She tried Em again, but once again the call went straight to voicemail.

"Oh, Buckley," she muttered, tapping her teeth. "Where are you..."

Chapter 36

Em was quickly losing her faith in Buckley's powers of persuasion. They'd already tried all the rooms in her apartment, and no wraith had shown its face. They'd been assigned the mission to talk to the remaining members of the Pringle family, in a bid to draw them out and to extract further information, but so far they hadn't succeeded in talking to a single one of them. Finley and Darren, the two brothers, hadn't responded to their pleas, and neither had Tawnya. Of course, it was very well possible they didn't occupy this part of the house, so they'd also gone into Darian's apartment and had repeated the procedure over there, but no luck either.

"I think they just don't want to talk to us," was her conclusion.

"Looks like you're right," said Buckley, carefully smoothing his gray hair over the large hole in his head. "I don't get it. Usually all ghosts like to talk to me. I can draw them out like that," he added, snapping his fingers.

"Maybe they didn't die here," suggested Em. "We should have asked Broderick for an exact location of the bodies." She shivered even as she spoke the words. To think that this house had been the scene of these gruesome murders still filled her with a sense of dread. "You know, Buckley, to be honest I don't think I can keep on living here. To know that all these people died here? I don't think I'm ever going to be at ease here again."

"It's all right, Em," said Buckley warmly. "Once they're gone it will be just fine. Their presence won't be felt throughout the house like it is now."

"If Broderick had believed in ghosts he'd never have bought this flat." She was sure of it. Whatever his faults, Broderick didn't want her to suffer.

"Why don't we try some of the other parts of the house?" Buckley suggested gently. "There are nine apartments, you say?"

"Yes, but I don't have the keys," she pointed out, and when Buckley tilted his head and gave her a kindly smile, she said, "Oh, of course. You don't need a key, do you, Buckley? You can just drift through the door."

"That's right."

She smiled. "It's quite handy having a ghost around, you know?"

"Thank you," he said graciously. "Why don't we split up? I'll check the other flats while you inspect Thorley's. At least we know who died there."

"Let's hope Etzel and Adele are in a talking mood," said Em.

They'd left Darian's apartment and she locked the door again, then proceeded to her own to ask Thorley for the key to his place. When she walked in, she was surprised to find him gone.

"Thorley?" she cried, and saw that her laptop was still open on the Skype window, but no call had been initiated. Weird. Why wouldn't he call Callesta? Perhaps she wasn't online, but then why hadn't he even tried?

She shrugged off her surprise, figuring he must have gone back up to his apartment. So she walked out of the apartment, right past her phone, which was lying on the table, and closed the door. Moments later she arrived on the top floor, and saw that the door was ajar. She smiled. Her hunch had proved right. Thorley must have forgotten something and had returned to his apartment to fetch it. So she pushed open the door and walked in.

She was actually glad he was part of their team. A strong, muscular man like him was great to have around, especially with two vicious killers on the prowl. And the fact that he was very easy on the eyes wasn't too bad either, of course. Though she had to admit that this entire ordeal had brought her and Broderick closer together again. It had reminded her of the sufferings they'd gone through when it was discovered they couldn't have a baby together.

The fact that they were perfectly compatible in their incompatibility had been the source of some wry humor, their own personal secret that they hadn't shared with anyone. Now, discovering that Darian knew, had been like a blast from the past. A past where Broderick had been her rock, and she was starting to think that perhaps she'd overreacted when she'd learned about the affair with his yoga instructor. Perhaps, like Broderick insisted, it was simply gossip and nothing more.

The first she'd heard about it was from Carmella Craig, one of her oldest and dearest friends. Now she was starting to think that perhaps Carmella had simply made it all up? She'd always had a jealous streak, and had suffered a recent divorce herself, her husband cheating on her with the housekeeper. Perhaps Carmella wanted others to suffer as she had suffered?

She vowed that when this was all over, she would talk to Caroline Freeby face to face. Find out from the yoga maven herself how much truth there was to this affair. She'd get it straight from the horse's mouth and be done with it.

She stepped into Thorley's apartment and called out, "Yoo-hoo! Thorley? Are you in here? I was looking for you downstairs but couldn't find you..."

The apartment was eerily quiet, and a shiver ran up her spine. She half expected Grandpa and Grandma Cromwell to put in a sudden appearance. She hoped they weren't the goo-spitting ghouls the rest of the family apparently was.

"Thorley?" she called out again. To her right was the room he'd set up as his private gym. It looked deserted now, the gleaming machinery providing her flashbacks to her own times at the gym. She might be in her fifties now, but she still had the buns of steel other, younger women would fight for.

She walked down a short corridor and next found herself in the living room which was... empty. No furniture, no furnishings... Nothing but bare walls and floors. This was so weird!

She quickly walked into the bedroom, and the same scene greeted her: no bed, no closets, no curtains on the windows...

She finished her inspection of the rest of the apartment and discovered that nobody lived here, and apparently nobody had for a very long time, judging from the dust bunnies and cobwebs that were covering the walls.

Apart from the gym, not a single item indicated Thorley Flax had ever lived here. And she was just starting to think that perhaps she was in the wrong apartment, that Thorley lived next door and only used the gym room here, when a figure came drifting through the wall.

"Well, Buckley?" she asked, an edge to her voice. "What did you find?"

Buckley looked around, and seemed as surprised as she was. "Nothing," he said. "Not a soul in sight. It's as if they're all into hiding or something. What about this place? Any sign of Etzel or Adele... or Thorley?"

She shook her head. "As you can see, nobody lives here, Buckley."

The old ghost stared around. "Are you sure you've got the right place?"

She hitched up her shoulders. "To be honest, I never even met Thorley before. When Jarrett brought him by that was the first time we met. I just figured he was one of those people who like to keep to themselves."

Buckley scratched his scalp. "It's the oddest thing," he agreed.

And as she headed for the door, the antiquarian simply disappeared into the floor. It was such an annoying habit, she thought. And so impolite.

She arrived back at her own apartment and let herself in with the key, Buckley already way ahead of her and floating through the living room when she walked in. And that's when she saw them: Thorley Flax, seated comfortably on the couch, accompanied by another man, who looked positively sleazy, a baseball cap on his head, his bearded face leering at her.

"Oh, hi, Thorley," she said. "Did you bring a friend?"

Thorley grinned. "You could say that. Em, meet Alistair Adair. Alistair, meet Emmanuella Watley. The woman who took in little Tanner Pringle."

Alistair's grin widened, and only now did Em see that he was holding a very big knife in his hands, and so was Thorley. And then it finally dawned on her. Two men, one thin, one big. "Oh, my God," she cried, her hands going to her face. "You're the Brunskill Manor killers! You killed the Pringles!"

"Bingo," said Thorley pleasantly. "And now we're going to kill you."

Chapter 37

Harry and Jarrett arrived just in time to see how two men were approaching Em menacingly. One of them was Thorley, the other was Alistair, who'd apparently managed to beat them to the scene. The men had driven Em into a corner, and she eyed them with her upper lip drawn up in a feral expression of anger. She'd grabbed a small vase, and hoisted it over her head, ready to throw it at the men, who were both armed with big knives.

"Hey!" cried Harry. "Drop your weapons!"

She'd heard the phrase used in so many cop shows it rolled from her lips quite naturally. Of course, in those cop shows the cops in question usually had the hardware to back up the statement, in the form of a gun.

She had no weapon of any kind, so when the men turned to her and saw that she was unarmed, and so was Jarrett, their grins spread. Just then, Em decided to use her only weapon, and threw the vase at Thorley with all her might. Her face was displaying her displeasure at destroying one of her nicer pieces of art, but she obviously valued her life more. The next moment, it simply sailed straight through Thorley and hit the floor, crashing into a thousand pieces.

Em yelped out in surprise. "You're... you're not real!" she cried.

Thorley grinned. "Oh, but I'm very real, Em. But I'm also very dead." And then he turned back to her, while Alistair approached Harry and Jarrett, switching the big knife from one hand to the other and back again.

"You don't have to do this," she told the mechanic.

"Yes, I do," he assured her. "And even more after that little visit you paid me just now. You were onto to me, weren't you?"

"No, we weren't," she said.

"You can't fool me, McCabre," he said, licking his lips. "Thorley told me it was only a matter of time before you found out. You Wraith Wranglers are much too smart for your own good. And now you're going to pay the price."

"Don't deny it, Harry," Thorley called out. "You knew the minute you spoke to Cicily what was going on, didn't you?"

"No, I didn't," she had to admit. These men obviously thought she and Jarrett were a lot smarter than they actually were.

"It doesn't matter," said Alistair. "You're going to meet the same sticky end the others did." And then he lunged at them, slicing the air with his knife.

"Why!" cried Jarrett, frantically dodging the knife. "Why did you do it?"

Alistair had them cornered, with nowhere to run, and Harry wondered where all the ghosts were. The ghosts of the people who'd been murdered by the same men who were about to murder them.

"Don't tell them a thing," warned Thorley. "They're tricky, and they talk to ghosts. They'd have discovered what was going on sooner or later."

"Yeah, that's not something we ever considered," said Alistair. "That two genuine Wraith Wranglers would come in here and start stirring up trouble."

"Stir up trouble! Us?" cried Jarrett. "We never stir up trouble."

"Oh, no? Then why did you come here in the first place, huh?"

"Because Em is my friend," said Jarrett.

"And mine," said Harry.

He waved his knife. "A bit of a coincidence, don't you think? For you to be friends with a woman who just happens to live at Brunskill Manor? I don't think so! Admit it," he growled, spittle flying from his lips. "You're working for Callesta, aren't you? She asked you to talk to the Pringles."

"Why did you do it? Why did you kill the Pringles? Money? What?"

He grinned. "Wouldn't you like to know, huh?"

"Wait, I thought you thought we knew already?" asked Jarrett, confused.

"Oh, but they do know it all!" cried Thorley from the other side of the room. "So stop talking and start slicing and dicing, Alistair!"

And he decided to follow his own advice by lunging at Em, who was now with her back against the wall. She cried out in fear, but then managed to dodge the man by darting behind the TV screen. The same TV screen where Leandra Pringle liked to hang out, only this time she wasn't showing herself.

And then Harry got it. The Pringles were all mortally afraid! That's why they didn't show themselves. With Thorley on the loose inside the house, they'd gone into hiding. So why had they started showing themselves now? But of course! Instinctively they must have felt that Darian was Tanner Pringle. So when he moved into the apartment a couple of months ago, he resonated with them and had drawn them out of hiding. Somehow they'd foreseen that the killers would return once they discovered who Darian was.

"How did you find out about Tanner Pringle?" she now asked.

Alistair grinned. "Cicily told us, didn't she? Said there was one more score to settle. One more Pringle to eliminate."

"So how did *she* find out?" asked Jarrett, who seemed disappointed that one of Zephyr Group's executives turned out to be a monstrous murderer.

"Dunno. You'll have to ask her. But now you never will!" he cried, and lunged again, this time almost nicking Jarrett, who yelped in fear.

Harry decided she'd had enough. Searching around for some object she could use to thwart this vile killer, her eye fell on a sort of large, hideous, egg-shaped object. It looked like a large brown egg, covered with writing that could well be hieroglyphic in nature. Trouble was, it was quite out of reach.

"Buckley," she whispered under her breath. "Now would be a good time to show you're a true wraith wrangler."

"Say your prayers, ghost hunters," said Alistair, drawing nearer now.

Murder was written all over his ugly face, and burning in his fiery eyes.

Chapter 38

Just then, a screeching Buckley suddenly reared up out of the floor directly in front of the killer and attacked the man. Alistair, startled, tried to skewer the old ghost, but dashed straight through him, of course.

"He's a ghost," yelled Thorley, annoyed. "He can't harm you, you idiot!"

But in the commotion Harry had quickly darted to the right and had snatched up the large egg-shaped artifact. And then she was lobbing it at Alistair, throwing it at the man with all her might, as one would a football.

Though she'd never been a practitioner of American football, she was a natural, for the heavy egg now connected with Alistair's head, which snapped back with gratifying force, and then the killer hit the floor, bouncing once on Em's sumptuous carpet, and then remained perfectly still, out for the count.

Thorley, however, was another matter entirely. That man wasn't to be deterred by any physical objects thrown at him, and when he saw that she'd taken out his partner, he cried, "What did you do that for, you pipsqueak?!"

"Pipsqueak?! I'm not a pipsqueak!"

"Wait till I kill you. You're going to squeak like a pig!"

"Squeal," corrected Jarrett. "Pigs don't squeak, they squeal."

"Who cares?!" cried Thorley. "I'm going to kill you all!"

"Ghosts can't hurt humans!" Jarrett pointed out. "At least not fatally!"

"For a ghost hunter you don't know much about ghosts," grunted Thorley. "It just takes practice, and practice is all I had for thirty-five years."

"How did you die?" asked Harry, genuinely interested, her brain working a mile a minute to figure out how they could defeat this killing ghoul.

"A stupid accident. We'd done the entire family, Alistair and me, and I was looking for that pile of gold Cicily promised us when I got stuck in a wall in Etzel and Adele's old apartment. By the time Cicily found me, I was a goner."

"So you've been haunting the ghosts of the people you killed," said Harry.

"You can say that again," he said with a grin. "And all this time I've been biding my time, knowing that one day we'd figure out what happened to little Tanner Pringle. And the gold, of course."

"What gold?" asked Jarrett. "There is no gold."

"Oh, but there is," he said. "We just haven't found it yet."

"So how did Cicily ever find out about Darian?" Harry asked.

He shrugged. "Simple coincidence. She just happened to run into some drunk one night, and he just happened to know about this chief inspector who'd taken in a boy from a murdered family. It didn't take long for her to put two and two together, and to warn us that our unfinished business was finally about to be finished."

"And that's when the ghosts started stirring," said Harry. "They must have known what you and Alistair were planning."

"Something like that," he admitted.

"I don't get it, Thorley," said Jarrett now. "You're such a... nice guy. Why did you do it? I mean, look at you, you could have been anything you wanted. You could have been the British answer to Arnold Schwarzenegger."

"Hey, I'll have you know I'm a big fan of Arnold," cried Thorley. His face had twisted into a vicious grin. "Let's just say Alistair and I have a taste for blood. And gold, of course."

"And for Cicily Pringle," Harry added.

He nodded. "And her."

"You were both her lovers, weren't you? You and Alistair?"

Thorley's grin disappeared. "She was never involved with that fool Alistair. We just made him think she was interested in him." He thumped his muscular chest. "But she was always mine, and mine alone. Only that stupid family of hers wouldn't have it. I wasn't good enough. So when she discovered those old fools up in the attic had a pot of gold hidden somewhere, she decided that the gold was ours, and that her family had to die. The plan was always for us to live here together, once she got her hands on the gold and inherited the place. And she did inherit, but we never found any gold, and then when I died trying to find it she vowed never to return here."

"How did nobody ever find out about you?" asked Harry. "Broderick..."

"That fool! Cicily was too smart for the cops. She simply told them that Alistair was her boyfriend, and he had a solid alibi through his mum, who vouched for him." He grinned. "Cicily had it all covered. She's whip-smart."

"Who would have thought?" asked Jarrett, more to himself than to the others. "A nice woman like Cicily getting involved with a murderer like you."

"Hey," warned Thorley, brandishing the knife. "Don't you

dare say anything bad about my heart's true love, you hear?!"

"What happened to Callesta?" she asked. "Didn't she suspect Cicily?"

"Of course she did," said Thorley with a shrug. "But she couldn't prove a thing, could she? We left no witnesses, except a bunch of ornery ghosts."

"One more thing, Thorley," said Jarrett, raising his hand.

"Oh, for crying out loud, enough already!" cried the muscular killer. "I think it's about time I shut you up. For good!"

At this, he stepped up to Harry and thrust the knife straight into her gut. Or at least he would have, if not at the last possible second Buckley hurled himself at the big ghost, and with a powerful effort managed to deflect the blow.

"Get off me you stupid little man!" cried Thorley, proving that ghosts could and did interfere with other ghosts. "Get... off me, I said!"

It was obvious that Buckley was no match for the powerful ghost, and in a last-ditch effort to turn the tables, Harry called out, "Pringles! Hey, you Pringles! Now is the time to fight back! Get out here, all you Pringles! Leandra, Anselm, Abigail, Tawnya, Finley, Darren, Jeff... Come out now!"

And to her elation, suddenly from all around it was as if the walls were coming alive, and then ghosts started slowly detaching themselves from the wallpaper. Hesitant at first, merely peeping their heads out, as if still afraid, but then actually and literally finally all coming out of the woodwork to face the man who'd murdered them thirty-five years before.

Chapter 39

"Did Cicily do this?" now asked Leandra hesitantly.

"It's not possible," cried another voice, and Harry saw that it belonged to Abigail Pringle. "Not Aunt Cicily!"

Two boys now also came forward, serious expressions on their faces. "Why did she do it, Mum? Why did Auntie Cicily have us all kill... killed?"

"For the money," said a deep sonorous voice, and Harry saw that a male ghost had drifted from the wall dividing Em's apartment from Darian's. This was Anselm Pringle, she knew. Cicily's big brother. "Thorley!" the man cried.

"Get away, you lot," riposted Thorley. "I killed you once, I can do it again!" And then he sliced his knife through Leandra, without effect.

The woman was staring down at the killer, tears flowing from her eyes.

"Cicily will pay," she warned him. "And so will you, Thorley Flax."

"Yes, we're not afraid of you any longer," echoed her husband. "You've been terrorizing us for more than thirty years but enough is enough."

"I'll terrorize you for thirty more," he warned, "and I'll add a few more to your number!" he added as he stepped up to Harry and Jarrett again.

"No, you won't," a steely voice rang out, and Harry saw that it belonged to the elderly ghost of a woman, and she knew this must be Adele Cromwell. "You've done quite enough, Thorley," she said, floating down from the ceiling. "We've been afraid of you all these years, hiding and cowed into silence, but no more!"

"Go away, you stupid old woman," grunted Thorley.

"Miss McCabre is right," said her husband, an elderly ghost with curly white hair. "It's time we rose up and put a stop to this madness once and for all!"

And at this, the entire flock of ghosts now descended upon Thorley, who screamed in panic as a dozen ghosts of his victims now took a firm hold of him and started dragging him away.

"You can't do this!" he screamed.

"Yes, we can," boomed the group, and then they all disappeared into a wall, dragging a screaming and kicking Thorley from view.

The last thing Harry saw was a dark hole slowly closing in the wall, and then the Pringles were all gone, and so was their vicious killer. The only ones who remained were Leandra Pringle and her little girl Abigail.

"What... what did you do to him?" asked Jarrett, visibly horrified.

"We're dragging him to hell, where he belongs," Leandra said simply. Then she shook her head. "He'll never bother us again." She smiled, and slowly drifted down as she approached Harry and Jarrett. Unlike the first time they'd made her acquaintance, Darian's mother was a vision of wispy white, not an ounce of green goo in sight.

"Thank you, Harry McCabre. And thank you, Jarrett Zephyr-Cornwall."

"Thornton," muttered Jarrett.

"You've given us the courage to take back our lives. Finally, after all these years..." Harry saw a silver tear blinking in the corner of the woman's eye.

Just then, the door swung open, and Darian and Broderick barged in.

"Harry!" Darian cried, running up to her and clasping her into his arms. "Are you all right?!"

"Em!" boomed Broderick, and followed his son's example by taking his soon-to-be-ex-wife into his arms and pressing her firmly to his bosom.

"I'm fine, Darian," said Harry softly, and then Darian was alerted by a voice, the voice of his real mother.

"Tanner?" she asked softly. "Tanner, is that really you?"

Darian looked up, and when he saw the ghost who'd slimed him, held up his arm in defense.

But Leandra floated down and placed a hand on his arm. "Oh, Tanner, how is it possible that a mother doesn't even recognize her own son? You look wonderful."

"Mother?" asked Darian, greatly surprised.

And then Abigail ran up to him and slung her arms around his leg. "Little brother!" she cried, though now she was, in fact, the little one.

Darian didn't know whether to laugh or cry, so he did both. "Oh, crap," he said between two sobs, and then he was wrapped in a tight embrace by the woman who'd given birth to him.

Em and Broderick stood watching the scene with teary eyes, and when Alistair Adair, still on the floor, stirred, Broderick gave him a hearty kick and the man was silent once more. The effort earned him a sweet smile from Em, who placed a kiss on his lips and wrapped her arms around him. It seemed that more than one heart was being healed today, Harry thought with a smile.

Then, finally, Leandra let go, and soon both she and Abigail were slowly dissolving. "Goodbye, Tanner," Leandra whispered. "Take care of yourself, and take care of Harry," she whispered, and then she was gone, and, after a final wave, so was Abigail.

For the longest time, they all stood where they were, not moving or speaking. And then they all broke into speech simultaneously, recounting the events that had taken place. And before long, Darian was on the phone with his department, instructing his people to arrest Cicily Pringle, the mastermind behind the Brunskill Manor Massacre.

Chapter 40

Alistair Adair, once he'd regained consciousness, was duly placed under arrest, and very soon Em's apartment became a veritable beehive of police officers reconstructing the scene and leading Alistair away. Of course nobody mentioned a thing about the ghosts, or even Thorley Flax, because that would have been ridiculous. But they all knew what had happened, and Harry's heart swelled each time she caught Darian's eye.

"I guess this means the Horrockses and the Marses can return," said Jarrett.

He and Harry were seated on the couch, after giving their statements to the police officers, and watching the men and women in blue do their thing.

"Yeah, I guess they can," said Harry. She still felt a little dazed.

They'd learned a lot in the past few hours. After Alistair had regained consciousness he'd sang like a canary, to put it in ornithological terms, and as a consequence Cicily, too, had spilled the beans. It appeared she'd held a powerful grudge against her family for not allowing her to choose the boyfriend she wanted, in this case Thorley Flax. And then, of course, there was the allure of the gold stashed away somewhere at Brunskill Manor. Or at least that's what she believed. From her the police had learned that rumors had always circulated amongst the Pringle brood that Grandma and Grandpa Cromwell were loaded, and that they'd stashed their wealth behind the walls of their apartment, not trusting the banks to keep their little pile safe.

She and Thorley had quickly decided on a plan of campaign. A campaign to live rich without the meddlesome interference of her family, and Thorley had brought in his buddy Alistair. The plan was both simple and evil: first eliminate Cicily's family, then find the gold. Which shouldn't be hard because she reckoned she'd automatically inherit the house. That way they could live like kings and queens, minus Alistair, of course, who'd simply been brought on board as muscle for hire and as a patsy in case the police got too close.

It was, after all, imperative that Thorley stayed off the radar, which explained why Cicily had told the police that Alistair was her boyfriend and not Thorley. But Alistair had proven smart enough to provide himself with an alibi of his own, graciously supplied by his dear old mum, and the five thousand pounds he got from Cicily for his efforts hadn't hurt either.

Unfortunately, things hadn't exactly gone according to plan. The murders had gone off without a hitch, and when the dust had settled, and the house had been released by the police and awarded to Cicily, Thorley had started searching for the gold. Until he'd gotten himself killed in the process.

Cicily had been inconsolable. Vowing never to return to Brunskill Manor, she'd still had the good sense to hang onto it, taking out a loan and having it turned into apartments. The apartment where Thorley had died had been left as it was, the wall carefully repaired, and a gym put in so Thorley would have something to do as he wiled away the time, incapable of moving on.

For it would appear, though she hadn't told the police, that both Cicily and Alistair kept in touch with Thorley, hoping one day he'd discover the gold. And keep the ghosts of the Pringles and the Cromwells in check.

And then one day she'd run into Gary Reed, and had learned that one final remnant from her past wasn't dead as he was supposed to be: Tanner Pringle, her little nephew. Quite irrationally blaming Thorley's death on her family now, she decided that Tanner had to die. So she decided to engage Alistair once again, promising him a sizable sum of money if he took out Darian Watley. And so the three former associates were once again reunited in the pursuit of a common cause, only this time the stakes were even higher, for to kill a policeman is not something one can get away with so easily.

"I still can't get over the fact that Cicily is a cold-blooded killer," said Jarrett, shaking his head. "Dad is in a state of shock! Everybody at the Zephyr group is!"

"I can imagine," said Harry. "I'd be horrified." She watched Darian as he stood conferring with his people. She'd been surprised that Darian turned out to be Tanner Pringle, but if he was, he'd gotten over it already, for he seemed back to his old self. Over the course of this case Darian hadn't merely discovered his real identity but also the fact that ghosts really exist, and that Harry and Jarrett's business venture had actual merit.

He now walked up to them and sat down on the couch, letting out a long stream of breath. "Christ, this case," he said, shaking his head. "It's everything I never expected and more."

"What part surprised you the most?" she asked.

He thought for a moment. "Apart from the fact that my name turns out to be Tanner Pringle and that I was born the son of a plumber?" He turned to look into her eyes. "A newfound respect for you Wraith Wranglers. You did a great job. Saving not just Em's life but solving the murder of my family."

"It takes a great man to admit he was wrong," said Jarrett soberly.

"And to top it all off, I think we just found that gold Cicily and her murdering friends were so crazy about," he said with a glance at his phone.

Harry's eyebrows shot up. "You did? How? Where? When?"

"Well, they found Thorley Flax's body, exactly where Cicily said it was, and just a few yards from where he died, a small metal safe. My men just called in a locksmith to open her up. Wanna tag along?"

"Of course," she said, getting up. This case just kept on surprising her.

They mounted the stairs to the top floor and entered Thorley's apartment. In the middle of the floor, a locksmith was working on a small blue metal safe, smudges of caulk stuck to the back where it had been secured into the wall. Both Buckley and Em were also there, and so was Broderick, all watching with bated breath as Brunskill Manor gave up its final remaining mystery.

"It's a very small safe," commented Harry. "It can't possibly hold a lot of gold."

"No," agreed Jarrett. "And I can't imagine it's worth murdering an entire family over."

"Whatever happened to Callesta?" Harry asked now. "Did you get in touch with her?"

"We did, actually," said Darian, his arms folded across his chest. "She wasn't surprised. Said she'd always suspected Cicily, but could never prove a thing, of course. Cicily had a solid alibi, even if Thorley hadn't."

"So why was he never a suspect?"

This time Broderick responded. "Well, the main suspect was Alistair, of course, but his mother swore he'd spent Christmas Eve with her, so that didn't help us. And Cicily was smart enough never to be seen with Thorley. Anselm knew his sister had gotten involved with some kind of musclehead, but had no idea who he was, just that he wasn't good enough for her."

Darian nodded. "Callesta was lucky, actually. In that she didn't live at the house. Cicily wanted her dead, too, but figured they'd better wait until the dust settled. But then before they could get at her, she left the country, consumed by grief, and effectively saved her own life in the process."

"What a story," said Harry, and glanced at Broderick and Em, who stood together, hand in hand. "Are they... back together?" she whispered.

Darian shrugged. "Too soon to tell, but so far the prospects look good."

"And are you guys back together?" asked Jarrett in a stage whisper.

Harry flitted a look at Darian, and saw that his lips had quirked up into a smile. Then she felt this hand steal into hers and give it a tentative squeeze. She returned the squeeze and leaned in and placed her head on his shoulder.

The locksmith had finally performed his magic, and the small vault clicked open. They all inched a little closer to the metal oblong box and stared anxiously as the man retrieved a small pouch and placed it on the floor, then folded it open. It contained a number of small items, and when Harry crouched down to study them, she saw they were five gold scarabs, with small diamonds for eyes, each outfitted with a tiny label, as if they'd come straight from a jeweler's. Darian picked one up and studied the label.

"It says 'Abigail Pringle,'" he read. Then he took the others, and read the names of the five Pringle children, the last one his own. Grandpa and Grandma Cromwell had acquired five gold scarabs, one for each of their grandchildren, and kept them in this small safe.

"There's an envelope," said the locksmith, and took it out and respectfully handed it to Darian, who opened it with slightly trembling fingers.

"'Dear darlings,'" he read. "'When you receive this gift we will no longer be with you. But know in your hearts that we will always be there for you, and will look down on you from the heavens, guiding your every move. As a small present to help you get set up in life, we have a gift for you all, a sign of our love and affection. Keep it or sell it, but always know that we love you dearly.'" He swallowed with difficulty. "Signed, 'Grandma and Grandpa.'"

His voice was wobbling dangerously throughout, but he managed to make it to the end. And then Broderick and Em wrapped their son in a tight embrace.

"If only Cicily hadn't been so greedy, she would have received her inheritance after all," said Harry, awed by this wonderfully touching gift.

Jarrett was examining the scarab. "Must be worth at least a hundred thousand," he said, scratching at the diamonds with his fingernail.

"Don't break it," Harry hissed.

"It's worth a great deal more than that," said Buckley now. "These are scarabs of the eighteenth dynasty, belonging to Thutmose III. They're priceless. Absolutely priceless!"

"Yes, they're very nice," said Jarrett, carelessly handing the trinket back to Darian.

Harry stared at the scarabs, glittering in the light streaming in through the windows. "What's going to happen to them now?"

"I'll have to discuss it with Callesta, of course," said Darian. "But if Buckley's right about their value, I'd donate them to the museum."

"Oh, I'm definitely right," confirmed Buckley, who knew a thing or two about antiques. "No idea where they got them, but my best guess is that they acquired them from an antique dealer. They're exquisite items, Darian," he said, tapping the collection with reverent fingers. "Quite exquisite."

They all shared a look. The scarabs were a symbol of the love of two grandparents for their grandchildren.

"I think they'll go into a special exhibit dedicated to Etzel and Adele Cromwell," said Darian in a ragged voice. "It's the best gift I can imagine."

"Or you could have them all melted down and sold at market value," suggested Jarrett, always the voice of dissent. "No? Didn't think so," he murmured. "Well, if there's nothing else, I must be off. Deshawn has arrived with my distinguished guests in tow, and I'm on the welcoming committee."

"Oh, right," said Harry, who'd totally forgotten about Mörten, Tamatha, Bruna and Ella. "Let's hope their apartments are now ghost-free."

"I'm sure they are," said Jarrett with a keen look at her and Darian.

"And I think I'll go back down," said Em. "Are you coming, Broderick?"

The stalwart chief inspector nodded, a happy gleam in his eye.

"And I..." said Buckley with a sly look at Darian and Harry, "... probably have somewhere I need to be right now. Adios, folks."

Soon only Harry and Darian were left, Harry holding a priceless collection of scarabs in her hands, its sparkles lighting up her features.

"What about it, Harry?" asked Darian softly, as he gazed into her eyes. "Want to give us another shot?"

"If you promise that you won't call the Wraith Wranglers a bunch of silly poops."

"Did I say that?" he asked with a laugh.

"Yes, you did."

He took her in his arms, and planted a gentle kiss on her lips. "I solemnly swear I will never call you a silly poop again," he said, "though I can't make the same promise for Jarrett."

"Well, he is a silly poop," she conceded.

"Yes, he is."

And then they kissed, and if Etzel and Adele were indeed up in the heavens, they would have smiled down on them, and so would the other members of the Pringle family, now finally enjoying an everlasting peace.

Excerpt from An Act of Hodd

Chapter One

*F*elicity looked up with a frown. She'd been deeply engrossed in the latest Jennifer Boiler book. Called *Hunky Dory*, it told the story of Vivianne Dory, illegitimate daughter of Rich Cash, billionaire owner of the New York Giants, and her passionate yet vengeful tryst with Taylor Hunk, the Giants' roguishly handsome linebacker, who just happened to be married to Rich Cash's legitimate daughter Fanny Cash. So far the story was extremely riveting, but that was before odd whirring sounds intruded upon her reading experience.

"Alice? Is that you?" she yelled.

When no response came, she returned to her reading and was soon deeply identified with the charming yet flawed heroine of Miss Boiler's latest romp.

When the same whirring sound reached her ears once again, she clucked her tongue in annoyance. It couldn't be her fiancé Rick Dawson, for the reporter was in New York right now for an assignment. And it couldn't be Alice's fiancé Reece Hudson either because he was in Vancouver shooting his next blockbuster.

"Alice?" she called out once again. "Is that you, honey?"

It would have surprised her greatly if it had been her best friend and housemate, for Alice had sent her a message only one hour before to let her know she was running late, as she was putting in overtime at the mortuary.

As far as she knew, she was alone in the house, or at least she was the only human present. She was actually glad to have this rare moment of peace and quiet. She'd put in a full day at the bakery, which was always a genuine beehive, and since she and Alice shared the house with Rick and Reece, it rarely happened that she had the place all to herself. She'd soaked for the longest time in the tub, spritzing scented oils with abandon, had done her nails, and now, taking the occasional sip from her glass of vino, reclining on the couch, her feet up on the footstool, she was really unwinding.

She darted a quick look over at Gaston, her big, red tomcat, but he was ensconced on the other couch, taking a leaf out of his master's book by resting peacefully. Spot, the ghost dog they'd adopted, was lying in his basket next to the bookcase, and Tony, the ghost pony Reece had been gifted by an old friend, was out in the garden, probably chewing on an imaginary blade of grass and thinking about nothing in particular. And she knew that out in the backyard their two chickens Eugenie and Beatrice would be scurrying about as usual, working up the energy to deliver another egg into this world.

The entire menagerie, in other words, was at peace and not in the mood to produce odd whirring sounds and disturb Felicity's rare alone time.

She shook her head, her red curls dangling about her cherubic features, and sighed. She was reluctant to put the book aside, for Vivianne Dory had just told Taylor Hunk she'd only seduced him so she could wreak vengeance upon her father, who'd refused to recognize her as his daughter after impregnating her disabled hooker-with-a-heart-of-gold mother.

With a frown creasing her brow, she rose from the comfy

couch and made her way to the hallway, where the sound seemed to be coming from.

"Anyone here?" she called out, feeling a bit silly to be talking to no one. But then again, she and Alice had recently gotten involved with a team of ghost hunters, so she knew that even when you thought you were alone, some ghost might be there. Ghosts were not a shy breed, she had discovered, and had a habit of popping up when you least expected them. They'd even had the gall to show up in her bedroom, waking her up in the middle of the night.

"Show yourself," she now said, her voice forceful enough to draw out even the timidest wraith. Felicity was a full-figured young woman, and both her voice and carriage indicated she wasn't one to be trifled with.

As if in response to her statement, the whirring intensified, and she followed it into the corridor, deciding to figure out its source once and for all.

Her eyes first flitted to the hallway credenza, laden with knickknacks and other paraphernalia and the very nice key dish Alice had picked up when they were over in England. It depicted Queen Elizabeth II, though whether the monarch would appreciate having her face act as a key receptacle she could only surmise. Then her eyes darted down, and she saw to her surprise that a small disk was hovering an inch above the doormat, neatly obscuring the face of Gaston, in whose honor Rick had had the doormat custom-made.

The first thought that entered her mind was that the disk was part of Rick's collection of *Star Wars* memorabilia. It looked like a small spaceship of some kind, though why she thought this was hard to put into words. Perhaps because a closer scrutiny brought home the fact that the disk was... spinning.

She stared at the object, and wondered why on earth Rick would have left it out, and why on earth he would have left it on, for if this Starship Enterprise or Endeavor or whatever the spacecrafts on *Star Wars* were called kept on spinning much longer, the batteries would soon be dead.

So she stooped down to pick up the toy and switch it off. And it was then that the disk startled her by suddenly zooming up into the air as if yanked up by an invisible string, and practically knocking her on the chin.

She yelped in surprise, and abruptly stumbled back, landing on her tush.

She stared at the object, transfixed, and when a disembodied voice suddenly intoned, "Greetings, Felicity Bell. I've come to collect what is rightfully mine!" she yelped again, and this time more forcefully so.

Chapter Two

"Greetings, um, Han Solo," she said, figuring this was probably one of Alice's little jokes. And if it wasn't, her mother had always taught her to be polite and return a greeting with a greeting, so there was that. Then the import of what the voice had said came home to her, and she added, "Wait, what do you mean you've come to collect what's rightfully yours?"

"I am Severin Lobb, Allardian guardian, and I'm on a retrieval mission."

"Retrieval mission for what?" she asked, thinking that they made these toys so incredibly real these days. She wondered where the voice was coming from, though, as it sounded too robust to be coming from the disk's no doubt tiny and tinny speaker system.

"I am on a mission to reacquire the Ring of Hodd."

"Oh, you lost your ring, huh? Happens to me all the time. The secret is to keep it in the same place. Like a jewelry box? That way you'll always know where to find it." She eyed the disk amusedly, deciding to play along with the joke.

"The Ring of Hodd has been missing for close to eighty years and is presumed to be in the possession now of the fiend Mortdecai, whose sole purpose it is to destroy Allard and turn it into a living hell. If he's not stopped before it is too late it will be the end of the world as we know it."

"Isn't it always, though?" she asked with a wide grin. She was darting anxious looks around, trying to figure out where the voice was coming from. It was almost as if it came from inside her own head!

"You are a known associate of Mortdecai, Felicity Bell!" the voice boomed, clearly not amused, "and your day of reckoning has now come! You *will* denounce your dastardly ruler and surrender to me, or you *will* perish!"

She giggled. This was so neat! "Look, buddy, why don't you just show your face, huh? I mean, it's not very nice to talk like that to a lady and hide out in that, um, spaceship of yours, if you know what I mean."

There was a momentary lull in the conversation as the owner of the voice seemed to contemplate this. "You are right," the voice came back. "I will show myself to you."

She giggled again. Now this was going to be interesting.

But then, before her astonished eyes, there was a sudden shimmer distorting the air before her, like asphalt on a hot summer day. Suddenly the air was alive with dancing particles of light and swirls of a purplish mist. And as both particles and mist solidified and formed a definite shape, she scrambled back. Amazing, she thought. And right on the heels of this, a second thought: no way Alice is behind this. This thing has Hollywood written all over it.

And since there was only one Hollywooder on her list of acquaintances, namely Reece Hudson, it was obvious who was playing this little trick on her.

And as she watched, eyes wide and peeled, her lips parted in astonished rapture, like one watching one's first IMAX feature or a New Year's Eve fireworks display, the air was alive with shifting colors and shapes, until they morphed into the figure of a man. He was dressed in a gold skin suit with a billowing blue cape, straight out of some corny old superhero movie. He was handsome, with long platinum hair, a serious expression on his noble features and cool blue eyes locked on hers with an unwavering intensity. If she had to venture a guess she would have pegged him a youthful thirtyish, and definitely one of Reece's more weird actor buddies.

"Wow," was the only thing she managed as she stared at the apparition. Then, to make sure he got it right, she repeated, "Wow." Then she glanced around. "Reece! Come out, come out, wherever you are!"

"I don't know who Reece is," intoned the man, his tone grave and deep. "But I do know one cannot venture into an alliance with Mortdecai without harboring a deeply villainous disposition. And yet you seem so very wholesome, Felicity Bell. Wholesome and well-nourished, I might add."

She frowned at him and planted her hands on her wide hips. "If that's a fancy way of telling me I'm fat then you better apologize right away, buster."

"You would do well to apologize to me!" he suddenly roared,

sweeping up his arm in a threatening gesture. "As the official emissary of Allard's House of Hodd I'm sanctioned to use any means necessary to reacquire the Ring of Hodd!"

"Yes, well, that's all very well and good," she said, wondering who'd written this guy's script. It was a little heavy on the sudden plots twists, she thought, and though the guy was definitely a gifted actor, he was chewing up the scenery like there was no tomorrow. "But I don't have your ring, buddy. In fact I've never even heard of this Mortdecai character, except for the Johnny Depp movie, of course, which I thought was hilarious," she quickly added, in case he'd get all worked up about that as well.

The man was now lowering his head, glowering at her from beneath his brows. The effect was disconcerting to say the least, but she still felt he was overdoing it a tad, and was making mental notes on his performance to discuss with him later on, when all this was over. "We've long suspected that you were in cahoots with the nefarious Mortdecai and now I'm certain." He suddenly thrust out his fist, then spread his fingers. "Give me the Ring of Hodd or face the wrath of Allard, Felicity Bell!"

She stared at the empty hand, wondering why this ring was so important, but then figured the screenwriter hadn't had a lot of inspiration. So, with a sigh, she grabbed the first ring she found from Queen Elizabeth's face and placed it in the man's hand. "Here you go, buddy. Knock yourself out." It was a ring Alice had recently won at the Happy Bays carnival, she saw. Some piece of plastic junk with pink colored glass for a stone. She wouldn't miss it.

He eyed the ring seriously. "Do you vow this is the ring you have stolen? The ring with which you have helped set up Mortdecai in his own realm?"

"Sure," she said with a grin. "Whatever you say, bud." She

now wondered if this was one of those cosplay things. She'd heard a lot about it but had never been in one. "Now why don't you go back into that tiny spaceship of yours and return to Ashtray to free your rulers, huh? I'm sure they're awaiting your return anxiously." She uttered these last words in the same overly dramatic tone he employed, deciding to have some fun with it.

"I am glad you have decided to give up the Ring of the House of Hodd without a fight. Now you must renounce Mortdecai once and for all."

"Yeah, yeah, I renounce Mortdecai. This is so cool! How do you do it?"

He ignored this outburst, balling his fist and trapping Alice's key inside it. Then he shook it. "Don't repeat this foul and repellent behavior, Felicity Bell. Association with Mortdecai is punishable by death, and next time you entertain his presence in your realm, I will not hesitate to crush both you and your realm with an iron fist. There will be no mercy on my part!"

This took her aback a little. "Destroy my realm? With that silly spaceship of yours? I'd like to see you try, buster."

"Don't let the size of my vessel fool you! It is a weapon of destruction so powerful and sinister it could wipe out this realm in a heartbeat!"

Felicity wondered how he'd manage that, but then figured the guy was just grandstanding. She decided to call his bluff. "I don't believe you, buddy. You and that spinning casserole couldn't put a dent in this realm if you tried."

He stared at her with a deep frown creasing his brow. If he wasn't careful that thing was going to create a rut so deep even Silly Putty wouldn't fix it. "I see now why Mortdecai has chosen you," he growled. "You are a brazen one, Felicity Bell! I'm starting to wonder if your renunciation of Mortdecai was but a ploy to throw me off your scent." He held up the ring. "Is this even the Ring of Hodd or have you foisted some old detritus upon me? Speak, mortal!"

"I, um…" she began.

"By the powers vested in me by King Hodd, ruler of Allard and head of the House of Hodd, I issue a first warning!" he roared, raising his fist high.

Suddenly, it was as if a lightning storm broke out in the middle of the hallway. The ceiling opened up and dark, purple clouds swirled, flashes of light slashing the air, and then just as abruptly the world was plunged into darkness, a vortex opening up above her with a deafening roar, and then she was pulled up, sucked up into the swirling mass of dark clouds. And as she felt her body rising ever higher, it was almost as if she was being swallowed up into an entire galaxy that was housed right there in her ceiling. The moment she passed through the vortex, she could see stars twinkling, and then she was soaring, moving higher and faster with every passing second.

She yelled, "Reece, this is so great!" but it was as if her body had been sucked into a void, her own voice sounding distant and far away, and just as suddenly as she'd been cast away into her very own milky way, the bottom dropped out from under her and she was falling faster and faster, her stomach churning as if she were on a rollercoaster going down. She laughed and whooped at the familiar sensation of tumbling down from a great height and then, when she thought things couldn't get any weirder, she heard Reece's actor friend's voice booming in her ears.

"Will you halt all your associations with Mortdecai?!" he roared.

"Yeah, sure!" she yelled back. This was even better than Jennifer Boiler!

A hush fell over the world as silence suddenly returned, and as she fell to earth, her hair whipping in the wind, her cheeks fluttering, she thought this must be what it felt like to jump from an airplane! And as her body tumbled through the air, twisting and turning, she laughed loudly, then screamed with mirth. She didn't know how Reece had pulled this off, but it was way cool!

"Very well, then," the voice boomed in her inner ear. "Consider this a warning, Felicity Bell. A small demonstration of my power. If you thwart me again, or harbor the evil slayer Mortdecai, your realm will be annihilated!"

"Whatever you say!" she yelled back to the disembodied voice, and then, suddenly, it was all over. She fell down with a thump on the hallway floor, next to the credenza, and the ceiling closed over her with a soft Whump!

When she looked up, she saw that both the small whirling disk and Severin Lobb were gone, the return to normalcy so jarring that it took her a moment to catch both her breath and her sense of orientation.

"Wow! That was great, you guys!" she yelled. "Can I go again?!"

But if she'd expected Alice and Reece to pop out from behind a curtain to give her a high-five, she was mistaken. Instead, there was the scratchy sound of a key in the lock, and she watched Alice stride in, looking a little haggard after a long working day. And as she stared expectantly at her friend, it became obvious to her that Alice had had nothing to do with this.

Chapter Three

"Hey, honey," said Alice, wondering why Fee was sitting on the hallway floor. And why her cheeks were so red and her eyes so wide and shiny.

She threw her keys on the little plate they'd picked up in England, and checked her face in the mirror over the credenza. She thought her pixie face looked a little pale, and her blond bob a little lackluster, but then she'd just spent her day with people looking a lot less lively. In fact as unlively as you could get. Working at the mortuary wasn't perhaps her favorite job in the world, but it wasn't the worst one either. At least it was pretty peaceful. And it wasn't as if she had to do any of the gruesome stuff either. That was all Uncle Charlie's responsibility. She just took care of the customers—the live ones—and from time to time assisted her uncle in dressing up the stiffs.

Business was booming lately, with a spate of deaths hitting Happy Bays. The downside was that she had to work harder than ever, the upside that her bank account was feeling very happy lately, with all the cashola flowing in.

Only now did she notice that Fee was staring at her, panting slightly.

"What's wrong, honey?" she asked. "Why are you looking at me like that?"

"Either you just played the most elaborate trick on me," said Fee, "or I just got a visit from an emissary of Allard called Severin Lobb who said he was going to destroy me and my realm if I didn't hand him back the Ring of Hodd and cease all cooperation with a guy named Mortdecai, an evil being intent on destroying Allard's rightful rulers and their world."

Alice stared at her friend, trying to process this. She knew Fee as just about the most levelheaded person on her very short list of friends and acquaintances, and this frankly wasn't the Fee she knew and loved. "Allard? Severin Lobb? Mortdecai? What the heck are you talking about, hon?" she asked, walking past her friend and into the living room. Frankly she was starving, and could use a slice of pizza or a chicken wing around now.

Fee followed her into the living room, after darting anxious glances around, as if fully expecting something or someone to pop up out of the blue.

"Did you and Reece hire an actor and George Lucas's Industrial Light and Magic to play this trick on me or am I just plain losing my mind?"

Alice laughed. "As if I've got the time or energy to set up something like that. Why? Some guy show up with a singing telegram just now?"

Fee stared at her. "If it wasn't you... Maybe it was Reece?"

"Don't think so, Fee. Reece is on location in Vancouver. Some science fiction extravaganza. Even gets to wear a spacesuit and everything."

Fee eyed her intently. "This Severin Lobb was a spaceman."

They shared a grin. "So it was Reece, huh?" Then her face fell. "But why didn't he wait until I was here?!"

"Maybe he messed up the timing?"

"Oh, crap," she said, rooting around in the fridge. "I hope he'll be back."

"Oh, he definitely will," said Fee. "I gave him your carnival key."

Alice laughed. "Good thinking." She found an old piece of

garlic bread and shoved it onto a plate and into the microwave.

Immediately, Fee took it out again, and said, "I'll cook you something. You must be starving."

"Well, I am," she admitted, giving her friend a grateful half-hug. Then she plunked down on the couch and saw the upturned Jennifer Boiler. "You started on the book already? How is it?"

"Not as good as Reece's actor friend. You should have seen it. The special effects were amazing! Almost as if I was in Disneyland or something."

She wondered why Reece hadn't told her about his big surprise, but then that was Reece for you; he loved to play tricks on people. She just hoped next time he'd tell his buddy to wait until she was home to enjoy the show.

Moments later, Fee had whipped up a plate of spaghetti with her very own extra-special sauce, and Alice was happily ladling it up. They were both seated in front of the TV now, and while some dumb old horror movie played, Fee told her all about this recent adventure.

"I don't know how he did it," she gushed, flapping her arms. "I mean, it was as if I was actually flying, up there in the milky way or something. And then I was being dumped back on earth. It was an amazing experience."

"He must have spent a fortune," said Alice between two scoops of pasta.

"Yeah, well, he can afford it. How much is he getting paid for this new movie? Ten, twenty, thirty?"

"No idea, but I'll bet it's a lot!"

"I think he can afford to hire a guy to look like Legolas and turn our house into a Disney ride."

"He looked like Legolas?"

"I think so. He's the one who gets to be the king, right?"

"No, that's Aragorn, silly."

"Well, he looked like Aragorn but with Legolas hair, then."

"Wow," said Alice under her breath, and stared at the screen, where a big, hairy monster that looked as if it was made out of papier-mâché was attacking the heroine, who was screaming her head off.

"I didn't see any wires, though, or any other equipment." Fee shook her head and leaned back against the couch pillow. "I don't know how he did it."

"They've got ways," Alice opined. "They're Hollywood, remember?"

"Yeah, but it was like I was really flying. It was amazing."

"Did you take pictures?"

Fee laughed. "Pictures? Are you kidding me? I was too busy flying!"

"You should have taken a selfie with this Severin Lobb guy. Put it up on our Facebook page."

Fee leveled a skeptical look at her. "I'll ask him next time I see him."

"We need to spruce up our Facebook page, remember?"

"Of course I remember, but I don't think our customers are into guys in gold tights."

"Everybody is into guys in tights, honey."

Alice and Fee had decided to expand Bell's Bakery & Tea Room into cyberspace by establishing an online presence. As an experiment they now sold cookies and other pastry online, and so far the orders were pouring in.

Fee had long done a regular baking column in the Happy Bays Gazette, and a YouTube channel to go along with it, and they'd recently started that up again, in connection with the online store. They had a Facebook page and a Twitter feed but the only thing missing, in Alice's opinion, was some juicy content to keep the masses entertained and coming back for more.

A man in gold tights doing all kinds of acrobatics was all they needed.

"I wonder what he meant by realm," Fee now mused.

"Huh?" she asked, pulling her mind back from picturing men in tights.

"Realm. He said he was going to destroy our realm if I didn't cease my association with this Mortdecai, whoever he is."

"Johnny Depp," stated Alice. "I actually liked that movie. Very funny."

"No, it wasn't Johnny Depp. I asked him and he didn't seem to like it."

"Must be one of Reece's friends with very little sense of humor, then."

"Must be."

"Did you ship out those orders? And put up the new prices?" Alice asked, wrenching the conversation back into the more materialistic realm.

"Yep, done and done."

"What did your mom say about this new venture of ours?"

Fee shrugged. "Mom doesn't know why people can't just come into the store. Why they have to order online in the first place. Plus, she's afraid we're going to burn ourselves out by taking on more than we can handle."

Alice laughed. "Burn ourselves out? Where did she get that?"

"Beats me. She must have read it in some women's magazine at Rita's."

Rita was Fee's mom's hairdresser. She liked to experiment with color, and had just managed to turn Bianca Bell's hair a very vivid aquamarine.

"Mom says if we're not careful we'll catch a burnout," Fee grinned.

"Catch a burnout. I didn't know they were infectious."

"She seems to think so. Says they're all the rage these days."

"Everybody's burning out, huh?"

"Guess so."

They were interrupted by a loud blaring sound from the TV and they both jumped. "Jeez!" cried Alice. "Did you sit on the remote again?"

"No, I did not!"

"Because your bum always seems to select the Cooking Channel."

"It does not!"

"Silence!" suddenly boomed a male voice. It echoed through the room like a minor gas explosion, and with the same devastating effect on both women. "You tricked me, Felicity Bell!" the voice thundered. "And now the wrath of Allard is upon you!"

Chapter Four

Alice and Fee shared a look of confusion, and Fee thought she could detect in her friend's eyes a definite gleam of excitement. But then Alice started rooting around for her smartphone so she could take a selfie once the man in tights showed his face.

"What do you mean, I tricked you?" Fee asked, just to stall things.

"The ring you gave me is not the Ring of Hodd! It is just a piece of junk!"

"Yes, well, it's the only ring you're gonna get!" said Fee with a grin.

"I warned you!" the voice rumbled, and then suddenly lights flashed and the ceiling opened, drawing surprised yelps from both Alice and Fee. "I will give you one last chance, Felicity Bell. Hand over the Ring of Hodd now or suffer the wrath of Allard's first defender!" the voice went on as the ceiling turned into a roiling, swirling mass of purple, lights flashing and thunder rumbling dangerously. And then suddenly rain poured down, instantly drenching the two women! They cried out in surprise, and Fee quickly took her Jennifer Boiler book and shoved it under the sofa so it wouldn't get wet.

In spite of Alice's enthusiasm, this was taking things a little too far, she felt. "Look, buddy. Enough with the waterworks already! You're gonna ruin this entire house! Reece? Are you up there? Can you tell him to turn it off?"

"It's just a trick!" hissed Alice, her face displaying her glee. "It's not real water, hon. I'll bet it's some kind of special water that doesn't make you wet!"

"It's making me pretty wet right now!" Fee hissed back, her hair now plastered to her face and her clothes to her body.

"This is the end of Allard if you do not comply," the voice of Severin Lobb droned one, "and I for one will not stand idly by while you destroy everything my ancestors have spent eons building! The Ring of Hodd! Now!"

"He seems very fixated on this ring," whispered Alice.

"Yeah, it's like a real obsession with this guy."

"He must have watched *The Lord of the Rings* one too many times!"

"I wish he would just show his face. I'm sure you'll recognize him."

"I recognize his voice!" said Alice. "It's Reece, I'm sure of it!"

"No way!"

"I'd recognize his voice anywhere! He's using some kind of voice altering equipment. Like autotune or something. Trust me, it's Reece, all right."

"What are you whispering about?!" the voice demanded. "The ring!"

Alice quickly slipped a ring from her finger and thrust it into Fee's hand. "Here. Just give him this. I'm sure he'll love it."

Fee approached the TV set hesitantly, holding up the ring.

"Here," she said meekly. "Here, oh noble one. Accept the ring I stole."

"Why did you steal it? Why did you try to destroy the Allard realm?"

Helpfully, Alice whispered, "Tell him you just love to destroy stuff!"

"That's right," said Fee. "Destroying realms is just my thing. I love it!"

There was a meaningful silence from the other end, then the voice came back, "You'll rue the day you went into an allegiance with Mortdecai."

The ring was suddenly snapped from Fee's fingers, and a smattering of sparks flew from her fingers as it did. She shook her head and muttered, "Amazing." How the heck was Reece doing all of this? She quickly returned to the couch and together with Alice watched as the ceiling swirled, almost as if the hand of God himself could at any moment reach down and touch them. Or smite them, of course, if this guy discovered that this ring, too, was a dud.

"I will be back!" the voice announced ominously. "And if once again you have tricked me…"

He didn't complete the sentence but the threat was pretty much implied in the dot-dot-dot at the end. They would rue the day they'd played fast and loose with the guy, that much was obvious from these last words.

Then Alice cried out, "Give my regards to Allard, buddy!"

But the voice apparently thought he'd said what he'd come to say and said no more, and slowly the rain lessened to a trickle, and then the clouds dispersed and the ceiling returned to normal, apart from a few big wet spots.

Alice walked over to the TV and checked behind it. "Pretty neat, huh?" she asked, enthusiasm making her voice skip into a higher register.

"I don't know how he does it," said Fee, shaking her head. Though she definitely wished he hadn't ruined things by turning on the sprinklers.

"I just wished he'd taken me flying, like he did with you!"

"Yeah, he left that part out this time. Maybe he'd reached his budget."

"Oh, man," said Alice with a happy sigh. "You were right. That was amazing!"

"I just hope you're right about this being Reece. Or else we've just signed the death warrant of our realm. What ring did I just give him, by the way?"

Alice grinned. "One of my Hello Kitty rings. And I've got plenty more."

Chapter Five

The next morning saw Alice and Fee busy at work as another day announced itself with its customary sunny splendor. Summer in Happy Bays was always a fun affair, and especially after the early morning traffic congestion had waned, all the workers working and the students studying and streets free for the shoppers to shop and the street sweepers to sweep.

On Gardenia Radcliffe all this business was completely lost. First her husband had lost his car keys and had to take the train to work, then her son Samuel had decided to stay home today. Officially because he was feeling a little under the weather, but more likely because he was being bullied at his new school. And on top of that her boss had called to tell she didn't have to come in today, or any other day, for that matter, for she was being let go.

Apparently he'd found himself a secretary more willing to succumb to his fatal charm, whereas Gardenia had always played extremely hard to get.

She now stood waiting in line at the butcher's shop, staring straight ahead of her. All of this had happened in the space of one hour that morning, and she was still feeling dazed and more or less shell-shocked. So when finally it was her turn, she couldn't even remember what she'd come there to buy.

She was a diffident woman, and to the casual observer looked very plain indeed; her face was plain, her hair was plain, her body was plain, even her voice was plain. To all intents and purposes she was as plain as could be.

Jackie Bouchard, the butcher's wife, who was more Mae West than Plain Jane, rolled her expressive eyes, but her husband Bud was more forgiving. He was even kind enough to tell her to take her time to gather her thoughts, and made the useful suggestion in future to bring a shopping list. "Makes things so much easier for everyone," he said with a friendly smile. And of course she agreed, except that in her situation shopping lists weren't going to make her evil boss go away, or the nasty bully pounding her son, or the mechanic who kept screwing up their car while asking top dollar to fix it.

Finally she stepped from the store, half a pound of chopped liver clutched under her arm, even though she didn't even like chopped liver and neither did her husband Roy or her son. She started walking, still staring straight ahead, her mind a blank, when she tripped on a piece of badly constructed pavement and hit her knee hard, scraping it in the process.

At the last elections Mayor MacDonald had promised his constituents that he was going to have the downtown area repaved, but as often happened with politicians, once reelected he'd suffered a memory lapse and the paving stones in certain streets still jutted out at odd angles, surprising pedestrians and forcing them to be vigilant and lift their feet high. In the interest of the community's mental and physical acuity there were certain advantages to this sad state of affairs, but for Gardenia, still dazed and confused after the triple bombshell of that morning, it was the last straw.

She was picking herself and her groceries from the ground when a helpful hand reached down and pulled her back to her feet, and when she looked up she saw that the hand belonged to Mabel Stokely, the mayor's secretary.

"You have to watch your step around here," said Mabel kindly. She was an eternally chipper woman, though there was a hint of steel lurking behind those kind eyes. Mabel wasn't a woman to be trifled with, and it was obvious she wouldn't be caught tripping over some silly stone. Her Nana Mouskouri glasses flashed as she gave Gardenia a closely scrutinizing look. For some reason that Gardenia didn't understand, the woman's hair had a deeply pink tinge, and combined with its fluffy aspect it resembled cotton candy.

"Yes," she now said. "Yes, this part of the street is a little tricky to navigate." Then she cast down her eyes, and made to hurry along. She wasn't in the mood for small talk, or to be scrutinized by curious mayoral secretaries. She just wanted to get home and have a good cry.

But Mabel was like a dog with a bone. Once she dug her teeth in she wasn't likely to let go.

"Oh, but you hurt yourself!" she now exclaimed, catching sight of Gardenia's scraped knee. "You should have that taken care of, honey."

"Yeah, I'll put some iodine on it when I get home," she said with a shrug. "It's nothing, really," she added when Mabel kept tut-tutting and tsk-tsking and studying her knee as if it was some long-lost Monet, Manet or Renoir.

"Why don't you let me take care of that for you?" Mabel suggested. "I live right around the corner."

For some reason, though for the life of her she didn't know why, she suddenly thought this wasn't such a bad idea, and followed the matronly woman to her homestead.

"I know you live outside of town and you really shouldn't walk around like that. It might get infected."

"Do you—do you have the time?" she asked. "I know how busy you are."

But the secretary waved a deprecating hand. "Oh, nonsense. I'm on my break anyway, and Happy Bays isn't going to fall apart just because I'm away from my desk for a couple of minutes now is it?"

Gardenia had the distinct impression Mabel thought it would, actually, and perhaps she was right. As the mayor's right-hand woman, she pretty much *was* Happy Bays, even more so than the mayor himself, Gardenia knew. For Mabel had seen so many mayors come and go that by now she was the rock all these elected officials leaned on when mapping out their ideas for the future of the bucolic little Long Island town.

"This is so nice of you," she said softly as she tripped along, trying to keep up with Mabel's vigorous pace. "I just hope it's not an inconvenience."

"Nothing of the kind," said Mabel as she dug into her purse for her key and then unlocked the door of her house to let Gardenia in.

She'd long been in the business of taking care of lost causes, taking in a bunch of stray dogs and cats over the years, and had once even harbored a stray parrot. To her Gardenia was probably simply another stray she brought in from the street to take care of. And then there was the fact that she was a member of the Happy Bays Neighborhood Watch Committee and thus imbued with a strong sense of civic pride, making sure the streets of her town were safe, as were its citizens. In all likelihood she took the state of the town pavements as a personal affront and its victims as her personal responsibility.

"I haven't seen you in town for a while," she now said as she pointed at a chair in the kitchen while she took out a bulky first-aid kit from the top shelf of one of the cabinets. "How are you and Roy? And Sam, of course," she said conversationally. "A big strapping boy he is. You must be so proud of him."

Gardenia swallowed, then nodded quickly. "Fine," she managed to squeeze out. "We're all perfectly fine."

"You don't look fine to me," said Mabel critically. "Are you sure everything is all right, Gardenia? You seem a little out of sorts this morning."

Finally she broke down and heaved a loud sob. She simply couldn't help it. Mabel being so nice to her brought it out, and then suddenly, before she could stop, she was pouring her lament into the secretary's ear. How Sam was being terrorized by a bully. How she'd just lost her job that morning because her horrible boss had decided she wasn't pretty enough and wasn't wearing her skirts short enough and her blouses low-necked enough. And how Roy was so stressed out lately from work that he resembled more a cast member of *The Walking Dead* than the kind man she'd married thirteen years ago.

Mabel tsk-tsked even more this time, even as she efficiently cleaned her wound of the pieces of debris, then applied some disinfectant and wrapped a crisp, white bandage around it. And as she did so, she told Gardenia she knew exactly how she felt. That a long time ago her own daughter Natalie had been bullied mercilessly, and how she herself hadn't been able to hold down a job for a long time, until she'd landed her current one. And that Mark, her husband, who worked as an engineer at the power plant, had had a tough time there at first as well, and had garnered very little respect.

"And just look at us now," she said, gesturing at herself as she washed her hands at the kitchen sink. "To think I went from lowly secretary to my current position. It's been quite a miraculous turnaround. A real success story." Her daughter had eventually blossomed into a beautiful young woman and had gone on to college and was now engaged to be married to a strapping young man, and Mark was now so respected at the plant that he had the director's ear. "Things can and do turn around in a heartbeat," Mabel assured her. "You just have to keep the faith and not lose hope, honey."

She nodded tearfully, Mabel's kind words doing her a world of good.

"Thank you," she said between two sniffs. "Thank you so much."

"There, there," muttered Mabel, and handed her first a Kleenex, and then the whole box. "Everything will be all right, honey. Just you wait and see."

When she left Mabel's house she was feeling a lot better already, and had one thing firmly planted in her mind: just like the mayoral secretary she was going to take care of her problems. And when that was done, she would finally be able to lead the kind of life a true Happy Baysian was meant to lead. But first and foremost she needed the right kind of tools to carry out her mission. And with resolute step, and this time making certain that the pavement didn't catch her by surprise, she set foot for Mick's Pick, every Happy Baysian's first choice when it came to loading up on guns and ammo.

About Nic

Nic Saint is the pen name for writing couple Nick and Nicole Saint. They've penned 40+ novels in the romance, cat sleuth, middle grade, suspense, comedy and cozy mystery genres. Nicole has a background in accounting and Nick in political science and before being struck by the writing bug the Saints worked odd jobs around the world (including massage therapist in Mexico, gardener in Italy, restaurant manager in India, and Berlitz teacher in Belgium).

When they're not writing they enjoy Christmas-themed Hallmark movies (whether it's Christmas or not), all manner of pastry, comic books, a daily dose of yoga (to limber up those limbs), and spoiling their big red tomcat Tommy.

Get Nic Saint's books FOR FREE

Sign up for the no-spam newsletter and get FREE reads and lots more exclusive content: nicsaint.com/newsletter.

Also by Nic Saint

The Mysteries of Bell & Whitehouse

One Spoonful of Trouble
Two Scoops of Murder
Three Shots of Disaster
A Twist of Wraith
A Touch of Ghost
A Clash of Spooks
The Stuffing of Nightmares
A Breath of Dead Air
An Act of Hodd

Ghosts of London

Between a Ghost and a Spooky Place
Public Ghost Number One

Witchy Fingers

Witchy Trouble

Other Books

When in Bruges
Once Upon a Spy
The Whiskered Spy
Enemy of the Tates
The Ghost Who Came in from the Cold

Made in the USA
San Bernardino, CA
20 April 2017